Also by Lin Oliver

WHO SHRUNK DANIEL FUNK:

WHO SHRUNK DANIEL FUNK?
BOOK 2

Escape of the MINI-MUMMY

Written by Lin Oliver
Illustrated by Stephen Gilpin

Simon & Schuster Books for Young Readers
New York   London   Toronto   Sydney

SIMON & SCHUSTER BOOKS FOR YOUNG READERS
An imprint of Simon & Schuster Children's Publishing Division
1230 Avenue of the Americas, New York, New York 10020

SIMON & SCHUSTER BOOKS FOR YOUNG READERS is a trademark of Simon & Schuster, Inc.
Book design by Lucy Ruth Cummins
The text for this book is set in Minister.
The illustrations for this book are rendered in ink.
Manufactured in the United States of America
10 9 8 7 6 5 4 3 2 1
Library of Congress Cataloging-in-Publication Data
Oliver, Lin.
Escape of the mini-mummy / written by Lin Oliver ; illustrated by Stephen Gilpin. —1st ed.
p. cm.—(Who shrunk Daniel Funk? ; bk. #2)
Summary: Still in shock after discovering that he has the ability, although uncontrollable, to miniaturize himself, and that he has a twin brother who is the size of a toe, sixth-grader Daniel Funk tries to focus on completing a diorama about ancient Egypt for his history class.
ISBN-13: 978-1-4169-0959-0 (hardcover)
ISBN-10: 1-4169-0959-1 (hardcover)
[1. Size—Fiction. 2. Brothers—Fiction. 3. Twins—Fiction.
4. Diorama—Fiction. 5. Humorous stories.] I. Gilpin, Stephen, ill.
II. Title.
PZ7.O476Es 2008
[Fic]—dc22
2007036641

FIRST
EDITION

For every single member of my beloved S.C.B.W.I.—you are my worldwide family—L. O.

To Brendan, for his newfound abundance of little brothers—S. G.

ACKNOWLEDGMENTS

Listen up, pals. Books don't just write themselves. Even I, the Funkster, get plenty of help. Like smart advice from the dudes and dudettes at The Gotham Group. And solid support from the super-fun staff at the SCBWI tree house. And inspiration from the fabulous Baker boys, who are role models for me and The Pablo. And without the big-time book brains at Simon & Schuster, there would be no book at all.

So thanks, everyone. We're some team, huh?

—D. Funk

Majorly huge thanks to the folks at Shannon Associates for their fishing expertise. I would be delivering pizzas or something without those guys. And thanks to those great folks at Simon & Schuster for picking me out to do this job. And especially to my mom and dad for all their support.

—S. G.

THE CAST OF CHARACTERS

DANIEL

PABLO

LARK

VU

GREAT GRANNY NANNY

THE CAST OF CHARACTERS

GOLDIE

ROBIN

MOM

GRANDMA LOLA

PRINCESS

PROLOGUE

Hey, welcome to my prologue.

Don't worry, it's pretty short. I'm just going to tell you three things you need to know before you read this book, and then we're out of here. Ready?

Number One. A diorama is NOT the same as diarrhea.

Let's be very, very clear about this all-important difference. A diorama is in no way related to diarrhea. The two words are not even distant cousins.

A diorama is something that shows a scene that happened in history, like the first guy walking on the moon or the Pilgrims landing at Plymouth Rock. Personally, I like to build my dioramas out of shoe boxes. You know, throw in a couple of Lego guys with swords and maybe some leaves or dirt and bamo-slamo, you've got yourself an instant diorama. Some kids, mostly of the girl variety, go all out with fluorescent paints and pipe cleaners and glitter and feathers and stuff. Take my little sister Goldie. She glued clumps of real broccoli onto poster board to make Robin Hood's forest. And my other sister, Lark, made a herd of African antelopes out of hair from a squirrel's tail.

If you ask me, and I know you didn't, that's diorama insanity.

Now diarrhea, on the other hand, is something entirely different. It doesn't illustrate anything from history, that's for sure. I don't want to gross you out with too many details, because we're only in the prologue and not even in the real book yet. So let me just say that diarrhea involves a toilet and an upset stomach and some highly unusual body sounds.

In this book, you'll never want to confuse a diorama with diarrhea. Enough said.

Number Two. I shrink. Not all the time, but way

diorama

more than your average sixth grader. Since last Wednesday, I've shrunk to the size of the fourth toe on my left foot seven times. Eight, if you count that time I fell in the toilet, although I refuse to count that because I'm trying to forget it ever happened. Hey, you try swimming in a toilet bowl and see how much you want to remember it.

Number Three. I have a twin brother named Pablo who is exactly as big as the fourth toe on my left foot. He doesn't grow or shrink, just stays his same old toe-sized self. I only discovered him last Wednesday, when I shrunk for the first time. He's been around

diarrhea

my whole life, but I never knew it. My Great Granny Nanny, who is the only other person who knows about him, tells me he was born in my ear.

Wait a minute, are you laughing? Cut me a break, will you? I mean, at least try to be a little sensitive to my situation here. If you told me that you had a secret twin brother named Pablo who was the size of your toe and hatched in your ear, I wouldn't laugh.

Okay, maybe I would. But I would try not to.

So there you have it . . . just like I promised. Three things you need to know and we're done. Prologue over. Listen, I hope it wasn't too funky for you. I've certainly been known to push the funk-o-meter to its limit. But that's how it is when you're Daniel Funk.

Oh yeah, that's me. What's up?

CHAPTER 1

The Funkster's Funky Fact #1: It is impossible for two people to see the same rainbow.

"Daniel, you're disgusting!" my sister Goldie called out as she ran in the front door, letting it slam hard behind her.

"Thanks, Goldie. Nice to see you, too," I answered in my best be-nice-to-little-sister tone of voice.

I was kicking back on the living room couch, watching some sports highlights on the wide screen, just trying to enjoy my Sunday afternoon. Until the Goldie attack, that is.

"Daniel, we have to talk," Goldie said.

Of all the words in the English language, I think those four—"we have to talk"—are my least favorite. People like my sisters (if you can call them people) always say it when I'm in the middle of something great, like a TV show or a video game. And who wants to talk then? Definitely not me.

"Take a load off, Goldie," I said, scrunching my legs up to make a place for her at the end of the couch. "Sit down and check out what happened this week in sports."

I thought my offer was spectacularly nice. Sometimes the nice approach works with Goldie, and you can get her watching TV and nip the "we have to talk" thing in the bud. But lately that hasn't been working so well. Goldie is seven-and-a-half, and now all she wants to do is act like our two older sisters, Robin and Lark. She imitates everything they do. So it wasn't totally surprising when she came up with that "we have to talk" line. They say it at least a hundred times a day. And trust me, what they want to talk about is never anything interesting like base-ball stats or classic comic books. Oh no, for them it's code for "Let's criticize Daniel."

My sisters are always telling me that I'm either dis-gusting or gross or weird or creepy. Or my hair looks like a bird's nest. Or I smell like cheese. Or I'm laugh-ing too loud. Or there's liverwurst stuck in my teeth. Their hobby is pointing out things that are wrong with me. They can't stand to see me relax. Actually, they can't stand to see me, period.

"What do we have to talk about, Goldie?" I asked, without taking my eyes off the TV.

"About how disgusting you are," she said.

I quickly checked myself out to see what was so disgusting.

Could it be my breath? Certainly a possibility. I

did have a tuna sandwich on garlic bread for lunch.

My feet? Definite likelihood. I confess, I had chosen my socks from Stinky Sock Mountain, the pile in my room where I keep what I like to call "gently used" socks.

My hair? Also a potential candidate for the disgusting list. I had worked up quite a head of sweat underneath my baseball cap at practice that morning.

Goldie marched herself in front of the TV, placing her body between me and the picture. I tried to look around her, but wherever I moved, she moved too.

"Furthermore . . . your friends are disgusting," she said, putting her hands on her hips.

I could tell she'd been at a meeting of her Girls Rainbow Club because she had a stupid rainbow painted on her cheek. Some club. A bunch of seven-year-old girls sit around by the canals where we live in Venice, California, and do rainbow dances and wear rainbow capes and take rainbow oaths. And they call that fun?

If you ask me, and I know you didn't, I think most girls' clubs are stupid. Clubs should have a point. Like, I'm in an after-school Simpsons Club, where my friends and I watch classic episodes of *The Simpsons* and eat snickerdoodle cookies. Now, that has a purpose. That's what I call a club.

"Be specific, Goldie. Exactly which of my friends is disgusting?"

"Your buddy, Vu. I just saw him and he said to tell you he's coming over soon."

Vu Tran is my best friend, who lives down the street. Most days, Goldie has a gigantic crush on him, so I was surprised that suddenly she thought he was disgusting. I mean, he does put a lot of gel in his hair to make it stick straight up, but other than that, I couldn't think of anything about him that was disgusting. I happen to know his parents make him wash his hands before and after every meal.

"What's so disgusting about Vu coming over?"

"He said he was coming here to work on your diarrhea. That is so totally disgusting."

"He didn't say that, Goldie."

"He did too. He looked right at me and said you guys were making some diarrhea together."

Okay, friends. Here's where I'm going to ask you to remember the prologue you just read, and the first very important point I made in it. If you recall, I strongly emphasized the difference between a *diorama* and *diarrhea*. I believe I was extremely clear about this.

Obviously, my sister Goldie had not picked up on this all-important difference. Which, by the way, is why it's crucial to read prologues. I rest my case.

"Goldie, Vu is coming over to work on our *diorama*," I explained.

"That isn't what he said, Daniel. My ears clearly heard him say that you guys were making diarrhea together."

Goldie wrinkled up her face so much that the orange and yellow stripes in her stupid cheek rainbow totally disappeared.

"It must have been Vu's accent, Goldie. You didn't understand him."

Even though Vu was born in California like me, his parents are from Vietnam and they speak English with an accent. Every now and then, I can hear a little of their accent when Vu talks.

"My ears do not lie," Goldie said. "They heard what they heard."

"It wouldn't make any sense for him to say that," I said, sighing. "People do not make diarrhea together. They make *dioramas* together. Which explains why we're having a diorama contest in my history class."

"You guys compete?" Goldie said. "That is so sick." She was refusing to get off the diarrhea thing, which is just like her. She can be so stubborn.

"And the winner gets to go to the All-City *Diorama* Competition."

"Whoever thought of that is the most disgusting

person in the world," Goldie said, "even more disgusting than Brandon Ross, who eats from the garbage pail and picks his nose with a milk-carton straw."

"Goldfinch Dove Funk," I said, "your brain is stuck on this diarrhea thing and it's getting really annoying."

By the way, I only use her full name when she gets on my nerves. That goes for all of my sisters. I mean, if you had sisters whose names were Lark Sparrow, Robin Flamingo, and Goldfinch Dove, I promise that you would stay away from using their whole names too. It's pretty embarrassing when the entire world knows your mom is such a bird nut that she named her kids after the feathered little critters. I guess we're lucky she didn't name one of us White Rumped Sandpiper.

I sat up on the pink- and purple-flowered couch that takes up a lot of our living room, and pulled Goldie down next to me. (By the way, here's a tip: When you live in a house of six women, like me, you can complain all you want about having a *purple- and pink-flowered* couch, but it will get you exactly nowhere, so you might as well get used to it. Forget the cool black leather couch—it's not happening.)

"Let me be specific, Golds," I said to her. "Vu is coming over to work on the diorama we are making about ancient Egypt."

"Oh," was all she said.

"It's going to be in a shoe box and will be something cool, like the tomb of an ancient king or a pyramid being built in the desert. Got it?"

She nodded her head.

"Okay, Daniel. I take it back," she said. "You're not disgusting."

"That's better," I said. And just to show her there were no hard feelings, I threw in a couple more details. "You know what, Golds? If we win and get picked to go to the All-City competition, Vu's parents are going to get us tickets to a Lakers game."

"Wow," she said, a big old smile spreading all over her freckled face. "Can I come too?"

"Since when are you a basketball fan?" I asked.

"I'm not. I hate basketball."

"So why do you want to go to the game?"

"I love watching the cheerleaders. Their outfits are sooooo cute."

All right, you guys. This is what it's like in my house. I live with people, girl-type people, who believe that the highlight of watching professional basketball—one of the sweatiest, hardest, fastest, most competitive games in the world—is checking out the miniskirts on the cheerleaders. Can you believe it?

"Goldie, tell me I didn't hear that. Tell me you didn't say cute outfits."

"I said it and I meant it," she said. "So can I come, Daniel? Please?"

"No."

"Then I take back what I took back," she said. "You *are* disgusting."

She got up from the couch, turned on her heel, and stomped out.

Sisters. I tell you, they never cut you a break.

CHAPTER 2

The Funkster's Funky Fact #2:
Dogs sweat through the pads of their feet.

The very next minute, Great Granny Nanny called me into the kitchen.

"Daniel! Come in here! I've got something for you to taste."

I didn't like the sound of that. She had spent half the morning forcing me to eat a whole pot full of boiled carrots. I was sure she had cooked up something even more disgusting now.

And I was right. When I went in the kitchen, weird stuff was brewing in there.

"Here," Granny Nanny said. "Try this."

"What is it?"

"Boiled baby carrot stuffed inside seaweed with five fish eggs on top," she said, like that was a totally normal Sunday afternoon snack.

She waved the fishy-smelling mess under my nose.

"Face it, Granny," I said. "The food thing isn't working. I already had a whole bunch of carrots this morning, and I haven't shrunk an inch."

"But I've added the fish eggs," she pointed out,

as if I needed help noticing those slimy orange balls oozing all over the seaweed. "Five, because you were born on the fifth of October."

"I'm not eating fish eggs. What if I give birth to a fish?"

"Never heard of such a thing. Only fish give birth to other fish."

"Well, I don't like the look of all that greenish-brownish grassy stuff either."

"It's just a little seaweed, Daniel. My grandma always said that seaweed and fish eggs were very powerful foods. That's why I mixed them with the carrots."

"Listen, Granny," I said, taking a seat at the kitchen table. "Fish peed on that seaweed, which makes it a big fat NO THANKS in my book."

"How are we going to find out what makes you shrink if you refuse to experiment?" Granny asked with a sigh.

She had a point there. Of the eight times I'd shrunk since last Wednesday, six of them had involved my eating Granny's goulash first. Naturally, we had thought it was something in the goulash that was making me shrink. The paprika maybe, or the carrots. But the last couple times I ate it, nothing happened. I stayed my same old, slightly-taller-than-average, size.

Granny and I both knew that we had to figure out what was making me shrink. I mean, you just can't go around shriveling up to the size of a toe and not know why . . . or when it's going to happen. That could be downright dangerous. What if I shrunk in the shower? I could disappear down the drain and never be heard from again! I'd have to live my whole life with those weird alligators in the sewers.

"Come on, Daniel," Granny said, nudging her stinky food concoction closer to my face. "Just one bite."

I leaned down and took a whiff. It smelled like seal poop.

Here's a tip: If your great-grandmother ever offers

you a hunk of seaweed with slimy fish eggs on top, run very fast in the other direction.

I opened my mouth a crack, held my nose and bit off a smidgeon of the seaweed and one fish egg. It was chewy and salty and squirty and . . . actually, I don't want to go into the taste now because I might have a barf-a-thon just thinking about it. Luckily, I managed to swallow it without barfing, although I did giccup once or twice. In case you've never giccuped, it's sort of a combo gargle, burp, and hiccup that actually makes your stomach feel great.

The Angel of Smelly Foods must have been watching over me, because right at that moment, the kitchen door swung open and my sister Robin burst in. Her nose twitched like a bunny's, but without the whiskers.

"Gross. What stinks in here?" she said. Then she saw me. "Oh, it's you."

What'd I tell you about the "Let's Criticize Daniel" game? They like playing it as much as I like playing video games.

"I do not stink," I snapped.

"Says who?"

"Listen, Robs, it might interest you to know that I shower *at least* once a week."

"I'd step it up," she said, "unless you enjoy reeking

like a locker room. Oh wait, you probably *do* enjoy that."

All three of my sisters like to point out that my body happens to make different odors than theirs. And I enjoy pointing out that yes, I sweat a good amount, but perspiration is the body's way of cooling itself and is part of the miracle of nature.

Robin, who's fourteen and a fashion jock, says she is totally not into the miracle of sweating. Yeah, no kidding. What she's totally into is the miracle of watermelon-scented lip gloss.

Lark, my oldest sister, who's fifteen and into . . . into . . . well, let's call it like it is . . . into herself . . . wrote one of her ridiculously boring blogs on her feelings about foot odor after walking past Stinky Sock Mountain. If you ask me, and I know you didn't, she went into way too much detail about my personal hygiene issues. Luckily, no one reads her blog but her. You can check out her views on my foot odor at I'm-a-know-it-all dot-com, but I wouldn't recommend it, unless you want to fall asleep instantly.

"Okay Daniel, not to be rude, but you have to leave the kitchen now," Robin snapped.

"Says who?"

"Says *moi*, which, in case you didn't know, is French for 'me.'"

The girls in my family think they run this house. I live with three sisters, a mom, a grandmom, a great-grandmom and at least seven female pets, including a hamster called Brittany and a bulldog named Princess. (Who names a bulldog Princess? My sisters, that's who!)

But I wasn't about to be thrown out of my own kitchen, so I took a stand.

"Am-scray," I said to Robin, "which, in case you didn't know, is pig Latin for *beat it.*"

Robin pulled herself up to her full volleyball-spiker height, which, I should point out, is much fuller than my non-volleyball-spiker height.

"I happen to have an earring emergency," she said, looming over me.

Without even waiting for an answer, Robin turned to the kitchen table and started to take out little boxes of stones and fake jewels and gold and silver chains that she had brought into the kitchen in a plastic bag.

"Who cares about earrings?" I said.

"Who doesn't?" she shot back.

I raised my hand.

"Well, that just shows what you know. Absolutely everybody loves earrings, which is why I'm making them to sell at school. We're raising money for our new volleyball uniforms."

"What was wrong with the old ones?" Granny asked. "I thought they were nifty."

"They're so last year," Robin said. "We all voted that we had to have new ones and that they had to be white with silver trim. Hailey designed them, and just as we were about to get them made, that guy who owns Pizza King pulled his support. He's giving our team's uniform money to the wrestling team instead."

"His son is in my class," I said, "and he's on the wrestling team. He walks around like he's the star or something."

"Once I was in love with a wrestler," Granny Nanny said. "Gorgeous George Malone. He had some pecs on him."

I laughed. Even though she's in her eighties now, Granny was pretty wild when she was young. Come to think of it, she still is. Just try riding on the back of her mint-green motor scooter and you'll see what I mean. She's got a heavy foot for a great-grandma.

"Wrestling is so gross," Robin said. "All that rolling around and putting your face in people's armpits and knee sockets."

"Knees don't have sockets," Granny pointed out.

"Whatever," said Robin. "It's still gross."

"Vince Bruno is gross," I said. "That's the Pizza

King's son. He refers to himself as Vince the Pizza Prince."

"Your little sixth-grade stories are so interesting," Robin said. "Now, could you leave?"

And that's when it happened. Bamo-slamo, just like that.

I heard the familiar growling noise coming from behind my eyeballs.

Then my nose felt like it was blowing bubbles.

My fingers started to buzz.

"What's that noise?" Robin said, turning to look out the window. "It sounds like wind."

It wasn't wind. It was my knees whistling, which is a sign that I'm going to shrink.

And then, I shrunk. Down, down, down to the size of the fourth toe on my left foot.

CHAPTER 3

The Funkster's Funky Fact #3: One-third of all the ice cream sold in the United States is vanilla.

By the time Robin turned around, I was gone. As least, as far as she could see.

"Where'd Daniel go?" she asked.

She was looking right at me, but she didn't see me. It's a known fact that when you're less than an inch big, no one sees you. People glance in your direction, but they look right past you.

"He left," Granny answered.

"Cool. That was fast."

Granny reached down to the pink linoleum floor, scooped me up in the palm of her hand, and dropped me into her apron pocket. Robin did notice that.

"What's that, Granny? Did I drop one of my earring parts?"

"No, it was just a little thing I found on the floor," Granny said. "It wouldn't look good on an earring."

"You sure?" Robin asked.

"So totally sure," I hollered up. "I wouldn't be caught dead on your stupid earring!"

When you're less than an inch tall and stuck deep inside an apron pocket, you can holler all you want, but trust me, no one can hear you. I should've just saved my breath.

Well, there I was, tucked into Granny's apron pocket next to a slightly used Kleenex and a lot of fluffy red dryer lint. Lucky for me, there were also some leftover crumbs from a honey-mustard pretzel. I gathered the lint into a nice soft pillow and settled in for a snack.

As I was licking the honey mustard off the pretzel crumb, I heard my sister Lark come into the kitchen. I knew it was Lark because she was flapping her jaws, as always. That girl even talks in her sleep.

"Would you guys like to hear the new poem I just wrote?" she asked.

"NO!" I screamed at the top of my lungs. Too bad she couldn't hear me.

"I'm reciting it tomorrow at the Women's World Poetry Festival," she said.

"GEEK FEST!" I shouted.

"And here's the best part. I'm going to accompany myself on the lap harp."

"NO, THAT'S THE WORST PART!!!" I hollered.

You haven't experienced true pain until you've had to listen to Lark recite her poetry. It's always about her feelings, and it's a known fact that she has way too many of them. I mean, she has feelings about things no one has feelings about, like toenails or superglue or cheeseburgers. I ask you, what is there to feel about a cheeseburger? You eat it, it's good, the end.

But as bad as her poems are, when Lark accompanies herself on the lap harp, well, it's way more than a guy can take. She straps that thing to her chest and strolls around, plucking it like a chicken. I don't know you that well, but I can promise you this: If you heard her, you would go running from this house as fast as you could and never, ever, come back again.

So when I heard the first strum of Lark's lap harp, and listened to her say, "I feel you, ice cream, cold on my lip with your choco chocolate chip," I knew I had to get out of that pocket in the worst way. I dropped the pretzel, grabbed onto a loose red thread, and started to climb.

When I reached the top, I stuck my head out and looked around. Robin was at the table setting up her earring workshop. Lark was strolling the kitchen, plucking her horrible harp and reciting her poem. Our bulldog, Princess, was hiding under the table, scrunched all the way into the corner of the room. Good call, Princess.

My grandma Lola had come in from her Native-American sweat lodge in the backyard. (What? Your grandma doesn't have a sweat lodge?) She was standing at the back door, swaying and tapping her feet. That doesn't mean the music was good, though. Lola teaches world culture, and she loves weird music from countries you never even heard of. Lark could have been playing the polka on an African thumb piano and Lola would be up and dancing.

"Granny," I called. "You've got to get me out of here."

"Ssshhhh," she whispered, trying to push me back down into her pocket.

I guess she was afraid that someone would see me, so she reached into her pocket, got her Kleenex, and tossed it over me. It covered my head and fluttered on the tip of my nose. It tickled. My nose twitched.

"Ah . . . ah . . . ah . . . ahchoooooooooooo!" I sneezed.

And before Lola could say "*I sveikata*," which is what Lithuanians say when someone sneezes, I shot back up to my normal size. Oh yeah. I forgot to mention that sneezing seems to have that effect on me.

I heard a giant ripping sound, and suddenly there I was, standing with my foot in Granny's apron pocket. My size-eight Converse sneaker had almost ripped the pocket off completely. I pulled my foot out of it in a big, fat hurry.

"Where'd you come from?" Robin asked.

"Um . . . out there," I said, pointing to the open kitchen window that looks over our backyard, where my mom's vet office is.

"And you suddenly decided to climb in the window because why?" Robin gave me a suspicious look.

"I didn't want to miss a word of Lark's poem," I said.

"It's about time you came to your senses and chose poetry over sports," Lark said.

Yeah, Lark. Like that's really going to happen.

"Oh Daniel, you're just like the *imbongi* of South Africa," Lola said, giving me a hug.

"I am?"

"Yes. They're men who are the poets of their tribes. I always knew you had a poetic soul."

"That's me, all right," I said. "Moon. Spoon. June. Tune. I'm a regular *imbongi*."

Showing off my sudden love of poetry was a great way to get the attention off the fact that I had just sprouted up out of nowhere. So I smiled and tried to look like a total poetry-loving chump.

Lark took that as her cue to fire up the old lap harp, which I took as my cue to get out of there. Somewhere between Lark's "Ode to Chocolate Sprinkles" and the always popular "Reflections on a Plastic Spoon," I slipped out of the swinging kitchen door and into the welcome silence of the living room.

Granny followed.

"Do you think it was the seaweed that did it?" I asked her.

"Don't know. We'll have to try it again to know for sure."

Man, figuring this shrinking thing out was like a giant science experiment. It was going to take time. I wished we could get help from someone like a doctor or a famous scientist. But Granny was absolutely clear that this had to be our secret. She didn't want anyone finding out about me or Pablo until she was sure she could protect us. Not my sisters. Not Lola. Not even my mom.

"Shhhh," Granny whispered when she heard Goldie come stomping out of her bedroom. "We'll talk later."

Goldie marched across the living room, sticking her tongue out at me as she passed.

"Basketball ticket hog," she said, and headed for the kitchen.

"I'd cover your ears if you're going in there," I called out.

As Goldie pushed open the kitchen door, I caught the sound of Lark's lap harp. Man, she was still going at it. She seemed to have switched from plucking to some pretty heavy-duty strumming. It's not easy to shred it up on the lap harp, but she was giving it the big try.

It was an awful sound, or whatever is worse than awful. Awfully awful.

I put my hands over my ears and made a mental note that when Vu arrived, I'd take him directly to my bedroom and avoid the kitchen at all costs.

CHAPTER 4

*The Funkster's Funky Fact #4: Wearing headphones
for just one hour will increase the bacteria
in your ear by 700 times.*

I'll bet you're wondering where Pablo was all this time.

Actually, I was too.

Being that he's only the size of my fourth toe, he's not all that easy to spot. He can disappear when he wants to.

While I was waiting for Vu, I went searching for Pablo. I needed to warn him that I had a friend coming over and he had to lay low. You don't really know Pablo yet, but I can tell you that laying low is not exactly his strong point. That kid is all action, all the time.

I checked out his favorite places in the house.

First, I looked in Goldie's jacuzzi. Don't get me wrong, my little sister does not have her own private jacuzzi. It's the one in her Barbie dream house. Pablo likes to fire it up and have himself a soak in his own personal spa, as he says. No Pablo there.

Next, I checked the turntable in Robin's room, which she bought with her birthday money during the five minutes last year when she thought she wanted to become a deejay. That was before she realized that deejays have to wear headphones, and headphones would give her the dreaded "headphone hair." She said she'd rather die than have squished bangs. She doesn't use the turntable much—it just sits there with the same record that's been on it for a year. So when it's not in use, Pablo likes to flick it on, jump on the turntable and go for a run. He says it's his own personal treadmill.

"Vinyl is cool, bro," he says. "Where else can a guy can work up a sweat AND listen to some excellent old-school hip-hop at the same time."

But the turntable was off and Pablo was nowhere in sight.

I went into Lark's room and looked for her mini-Webcam, which she uses to record her video blogs. (Oh by the way, did I mention they are deeply boring? I did? Sorry, I just can't say it enough.) Pablo likes to record himself playing air guitar. I tell him to be sure to erase what he's recorded, because if Lark ever played it back, our secret would be out.

"I love the erase button, dude," he said. "When I jump on it, it's like my own personal trampoline."

According to Pablo, almost everything in our house is part of his own personal playground.

Anyway, he wasn't trampolining on the erase button

at the moment, so I hurried down the hall to check out my room.

I kicked open the door and called out.

"Yo, Pablo!"

Whoops. That was a mistake.

"Did you say something, honey?" my mom said, sticking her head out from the bathroom across the hall. I almost jumped six feet in the air.

She was wearing a towel on her head. Oh wow, I had forgotten. Sunday is deep-conditioning hair day for the women of the Funk house. Trust me, you don't even want to know what that is. All I can tell you is that the goal is to have hair that's silky, shiny, and bouncy.

If you ask me, and I know you didn't, I don't see what's so great about having bouncy hair. I say if you want bouncy, get a ball.

"Hi, Mom. I didn't know you were here," I said, trying to sound totally casual.

"Who's Pablo, honey?"

"Pablo who?"

"That's what I'm asking you. It sounded like you were calling 'Pablo.'"

"You probably can't hear so well with the towel covering your head, and all that deep conditioner in your ears and stuff."

"Maybe. But I could have sworn I heard you say 'Pablo.'"

She wasn't letting this go, and I felt like she was waiting for an explanation. So I gave her one. It wasn't a good one, and I'm not proud of it. But it was the best I could come up with under pressure.

"Oh, that. I didn't say *Pablo*. I said . . . um . . . *knob low*. My doorknob is low. I never noticed it before and I just thought I should point it out. So I said '*knob low*.'"

She gave me a strange look, and I slid into my room real fast, before I had the chance to go on acting like a total moron.

"Pablo," I called in a whisper. "You in here?"

I walked over to Creature Condo Corner, the table where some of our family pets live. Pablo sometimes hangs out with Cutie-Pie, practicing his martial arts moves on her. Cutie-Pie is our Siamese fighting fish, and you can thank my sister Goldie for her embarrassing name. I originally named her Wu-Shu, which means "martial arts" in Chinese. The girl side of the family took a vote and changed it to Cutie-Pie. Pathetic, huh?

Yup. That's what I'm up against here in the Funk household.

I picked up Cutie-Pie's bowl and looked behind it, but Pablo wasn't there. Time was getting short. I needed to find him. Vu would be knocking on the door at any minute.

I got out a shoe box and took it over to my desk. It's the one I had . . . let's say . . . borrowed from Robin for constructing the diorama. On one side, it said "size 7." On the other side, it said "fancy jeweled sandal." Of course it did. What do you expect it would say, sturdy brown walking shoe? Never! That Robin is such a girl.

My desk was covered with a bunch of junk, and if Vu and I were going to work there, I had to clear it off. I chucked my math workbook onto the floor, my history book onto my blue La-Z-Boy chair, and shoved the stapler off the edge. I picked up the big amethyst geode that my dad had sent me from Peru, just before he disappeared into the rain forest seven years ago. I love that thing—first, because he gave it to me, and second, because it's beautiful. I like to look at all those purple crystals jutting out from the rock like sparkly little pyramids.

I don't know if you've ever lost someone close to you, but one of the worst things about it is that after a while, you start to forget what they looked like. Sometimes I pick up that geode and stare into it and try to remember my dad giving it to me. But the picture I get is pretty fuzzy. I remember he had big tan hands and a freckle on his palm that was shaped like a bear claw. And he always wore a brown beat-up rain forest kind of hat with a white feather on it. My mom, who is a major bird nut herself, says he loved eagles because they represented freedom to him. She says that's why he named me Daniel Eagle Funk.

As I carried the geode to the shelf next to my bed, I heard a voice coming from inside it.

A very small voice.

"Hey, bro. You trying to kill me, or what?"

"Pablo! What are you doing in there?" I said, squinting into the geode.

"Rock climbing, dude. It's awesome. Now put me back on the desk before I fall out of here and crack my head open!"

Quickly, I put the geode back on my desk and took a closer look. Yup, there he was. The Pablo.

I could just barely see him, wearing army boots from an old action figure of mine and dangling from one of the shiny purple ledges. He was being held up by a harness made from a green nylon shoelace. Hey, I know that shoelace! It was from my soccer shoes when I was on the Green Hornets. That was way back in second grade.

I had to get down real close and practically stick my nose in the geode so I could see and hear him.

"Join in, dude," he said. "It's tough on the legs, but the view from the top is so worth it."

"When did you learn to rock climb?" I asked him.

"Hey, I have to do something while you poor suckers are in school cranking out the long division."

He laughed so hard it looked like he was going to lose his balance.

"Watch out! You'll fall," I said.

"No problemo. I've got a harness—and a crash pad."

I looked down at the desk and saw a little circle of rubber foam about the size of a golf ball. It looked like it had been cut from the padding inside my Green

Hornets soccer shoe. Something was written on it, but the letters were too small to read. I grabbed the magnifying glass that I've kept on my desk ever since I discovered Pablo and held it over the letters. They said, "Pablo's Drop Zone."

I tell you, that Pablo has style.

By the time I looked up, he had started to scale up to the top of the geode. He was hanging by his hands on two purple crags and searching for toe-holds with his feet. Pablo jammed one toe into a crevice. Just as he was shoving the other foot into a toehold, his army boot caught on a jagged edge. He lost his footing and went tumbling down the face of the geode. Any sane person would have been scared, but not Pablo.

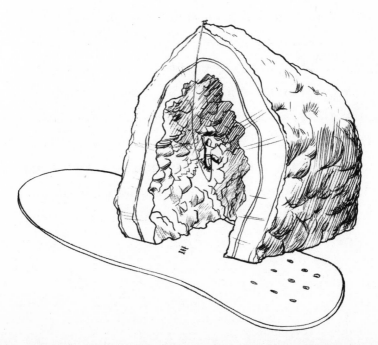

"Woo-hoo!" he hollered as he somersaulted through the air, bouncing against the edges of the geode. It was a good thing he had made that shoe-lace harness, because it stopped him just before he crash-landed on the desk. By the way, he would have missed his crash pad by the length of a ministapler and a pencil eraser.

He swung in his tiny harness for a minute, laughing and whooping it up.

"What a rush!" he shouted. "You got to try this, bro!"

"Looks like fun," I said.

I couldn't help thinking how lucky I was to have a brother who was so much fun, even if he was only an inch big. I had only known him for less than a week, but I already couldn't imagine life without him.

"Shrink yourself down and let's do it, bro," Pablo called out impatiently.

"I've been trying all day, Pabs. I've eaten major doses of carrots and even swallowed a fish egg. Something worked for a minute, but it didn't last, so I'm thinking if I tried—"

I was in the middle of that sentence when I suddenly heard a noise in my room. I turned around, looked toward the door, and realized we were not alone.

CHAPTER 5

The Funkster's Funky Fact #5: A jiffy is an actual unit of time, like a minute or an hour. A jiffy is 1/100 of a second.

Vu was standing at the door of my room, staring at me as if he had just seen a ghost.

"Your sister said I should come in," he said. I noticed that while he talked, he didn't take his eyes off the geode.

"I guess she never heard of the word 'knock.'"

"Okay, Dan, I'm just going to say it," Vu said. "I think it's weird that you're talking to a rock."

"It must look strange, huh?"

"Extremely."

I was quiet for a minute, hoping he'd change the subject. He didn't.

"Well, it's like this, Vu," I began, talking real slow, to give myself a chance to come up with a story. I had already done the "knob low" thing, and that hadn't worked out real well, so I was feeling a little short on confidence.

"I was trying to get ideas for our diorama," I said simply.

I paused and waited.

"By talking to a rock?" Vu asked.

"Exactly."

Here's a tip: If anyone ever asks you why you're talking to a rock, keep your answer short and sweet. The more you say about it, the more trouble you'll get yourself into.

Vu scratched his head, being careful not to squish any of his gelled-up spikes, and nodded. He didn't laugh. He just nodded.

I hope you have a friend like Vu. Maybe because his parents are from Vietnam and they come from a different way of life—maybe that taught him to accept the fact that everyone is different in some way. The point is, even when I'm acting weird, like I was then, he doesn't make fun of me. He just takes it all in and nods a lot.

"So . . . like . . . what'd the rock have to say?" he said.

"It said it was out of ideas, so I should ask the shoe box," I answered.

Then Vu cracked up. So did I. Unfortunately, so did Pablo.

"Nice comeback," he shouted from inside the geode. "Way to go, bro."

"Thanks," I said, without thinking.

"For what?" Vu asked.

Whoops.

"Um . . . for being my partner on this project. For coming over here. For inviting me to the Lakers game when we get picked to go to All-City."

"Just because I'm going to get tickets doesn't mean I'm inviting you. Maybe I'll ask Vince Bruno. His dad gets him front-row tickets to all the big rock concerts. If I invite him, then he'll invite me back."

"No way! You'd sell me out just to go to a few lousy rock concerts?"

"Chill, man," Vu said, laughing. "That guy is in love with himself. I'm going nowhere with him."

"Good. Just remember who's your partner," I said. "You'd better take me."

"And me too," Pablo called out.

"You're so little you don't need a ticket," I said, again without thinking. Whoops a second time.

"I'm bigger than you, man," Vu said.

It was clear I had to get Vu out of there. Pablo wasn't keeping quiet and neither was my big mouth. I handed the shoe box to Vu, told him there was no room to work on my desk, and suggested he take it out to the living room right away. He looked at the label on the side.

"Fancy jeweled sandals?" he read. "I didn't know you wore them. Don't they kind of clash with your baseball gear?"

Pablo hooted. That kid has a loud laugh for a toe-sized guy.

"The Pablo is amused!" he howled.

No, this was not okay. It had to stop right now. For sure, Vu was going to hear Pablo and come walking over to the geode and see him perched on his purple ledge, and how was I going to explain that?

"Tell you what, Vu," I said, putting my hand on his back and shoving him out the door. "I'll get some supplies and meet you in the living room."

"I don't know, man. Your little sister is out there."

I didn't blame Vu for being afraid. Goldie has a horrible crush on him. Oh, not a real crush, but the kind seven-and-a-half-year-old girls get. She's always asking him to play Monopoly and Go Fish and come to tea parties and princess proms. That's one reason he doesn't like to come over. Actually, that's four reasons. Good ones, too.

"I'll be there in a jiffy," I said. "I promise I'll protect you."

As soon as Vu left the room, I picked up the geode so I could deal with Pablo up close.

"That was outrageous," I said to him. "You know Granny's rules. You have to be invisible. Stay under the radar."

Pablo is not a big fan of rules—hearing about them or following them—so he changed the subject immediately.

"What are you guys working on out there, and why wasn't I invited?"

"A diorama," I answered.

"Whoa," he said, holding his stomach. "Now The Pablo is officially grossed out."

Okay, friends. Here we go again. Back to the prologue. Apparently my minibrother is not familiar with its contents either.

"No, Pabs. A diorama for my history class. About the ancient Egyptians."

"What were they eating that gave them all that tummy trouble?" Pablo said. "Must have been rotten fish in the Nile."

Once again, I found myself explaining that a diorama is not the same as diarrhea. Holy macaroni, is there no one in my house who knows the difference?

I didn't want Vu to come back in, so I quickly gathered up a few Lego guys and some colored pencils and glue sticks to take to the living room.

"What's this diorama of?" Pablo asked.

I told him that we had decided to build the inside of King Tut's tomb.

"King Tut!" Pablo said, swinging down to the desk so I could hear him more easily. "He's the Egyptian boy king, right? The one who became king when he was nine and died when he was sixteen."

Wow. I was surprised at how much he knew about King Tut.

"That's him," I said. "But actually, the ancient Egyptians called their kings pharaohs."

I confess, I was showing off a little. I mean, I had to know something more than Pablo. After all, I had been going to school since I was five, and he had only gone three days in his whole life.

"Those old Egyptian GUPS buried him with gold and jewels and servants and food and stuff," Pablo said, "so he could party in the afterlife. And then everyone forgot about him until one day, thousands of years later, some English GUP discovered his tomb filled with treasure."

By the way, GUP is Pablo-speak for grown-up person. So you might want to read that last paragraph again and see if it makes more sense this time, now that you know that.

"How do you know so much about King Tut?" I asked him.

"I heard about him when I went school in your backpack during your Egyptian unit," Pablo said. "And I thought being a boy king was so cool that I asked Granny to teach me all about him. We looked at pictures in her art history books and everything."

Even though we had only known each other for less than a week, Pablo and I are so much alike. We like all the same things. For instance, when Mr. Stout, my history teacher, told us about the discovery of King Tut's tomb, I thought it was one of the most interesting things I've learned in school. You have to admit, it sure beats the life cycle of an earthworm.

"Did you know that when they found Tut," Pablo said, "he was an actual mummy. You know, one of those wrapped-up dead dudes. How cool is that!"

"I love mummies too," I said. "I was one for Halloween in the fifth grade."

"Hey, bro, let me come out there and watch you build your diorama," Pablo said. "Please. I'll stay low. You won't even know I'm there."

"I can't, Pablo," I said. "Granny's orders."

I actually felt sorry for Pablo. In some ways, he had it great. I mean, he was totally free and never had to go to school or anything. But he must have spent plenty of time during the last ten years being lonely, too. It made me so glad that we had found each other at last. For his sake, as well as mine.

"You have to stay here for your own protection," I said to him.

"You're right," he said. "No biggie."

But I could tell it was a biggie for him. He really wanted to hang out with us.

"I'll come back as soon as we're finished," I said to Pablo. "In the meantime, you can go rock climbing."

He just nodded.

"Later, gator." I said.

He flashed me a little smile.

"Do your thing, chicken wing," he said.

And I was out the door.

CHAPTER 6

The Funkster's Funky Fact #6: The only mammal besides the human that can get sunburned is the pig.

By the time I got to the living room, Vu had already been attacked by the Funk sisters. The poor guy was surrounded.

Goldie was dealing up the Monopoly money and offering to give him both Boardwalk and Park Place for free if he'd play with her. Robin was modeling her earrings and asking him if he thought the green rhinestones went better with her blond hair than the red rhinestones. As if he'd care. And Lark had her mini-Webcam out and was interviewing him for the video blog she was planning to show at the Women's World Poetry Festival the next day.

"Do you think we're all born with poetry in our souls?" she was asking Vu as I arrived.

If you're dying to know the answer to that question, you're certainly free to read all about it at like-I-care dot-com. My bet is you couldn't be less interested, which is my personal position. I can tell it was Vu's, too. He looked like one very relieved dude when I appeared.

"Okay, all females hit the road," I said. "Vu and I have schoolwork to do."

No one moved.

This is what happens when I give orders in my house.

Nothing. Zip. Nada. Zero.

"Maybe no one heard me?" I said. "I have asked everyone to *am-scray*. Robin, you can translate from the Pig Latin."

"I know what am-scray means," Goldie said. "I used to have a pet pig, you know."

Last year my mom was taking care of a sick pot-bellied pig named Kevin Bacon, and he lived in our backyard for seven months. We all got pretty close to him. But I felt it was my duty, as Goldie's older brother, to clear up a few things about pigs.

"Sorry, Golds," I said to her. "This may come as a shock, but pigs do not speak Pig Latin."

That's all I said. Just a simple statement of the facts.

So why did she burst into tears and fling herself facedown on the couch, I ask you. Why? I swear, what makes girls cry is one of the great mysteries I will never understand.

"Nice work, Mr. Sensitive," Lark said.

"What did I do?"

"You embarrassed her in front of Vu," Robin whispered. "Can't you see that?"

"I told her the truth. You wouldn't want her to go around telling people that pigs speak Pig Latin."

"Honestly, Daniel. You don't understand a thing about girls," Robin said.

Guilty as charged.

"You are such an emotional clod," Robin went on, "that I'm not even going to ask your opinion about the green versus red rhinestones."

Oh man, she really knows how to hurt a guy.

"In fact, I'm going back to the kitchen!"

Yippee! What took so long? Bye-bye.

With that, Robin stomped out of the living room.

Yeah! Score one for the Daniel!

"It might interest you to know that the female soul is a delicate thing," Lark said to me. "In fact, I feel inspired to go write about it right now."

Then she got up and headed to her room.

Yeah! Score two for the Daniel!

Goldie dramatically pulled herself up off the couch, marched over to Vu and me, and started gathering up her Monopoly money.

"Thanks, Daniel. Now I don't even want to play," she said.

As she tucked her Monopoly set under her arm and turned to go, she looked at both of us and delivered the final blow.

"I may not ever want to play Monopoly with either of you again."

And she left.

Yeah! Score three for the Daniel!

Now that's what I call a hat trick.

CHAPTER 7

The Funkster's Funky Fact #7:
Camels don't sweat or pant.

True, Vu and I had left the construction of our diorama until the last minute. It was my fault, I confess. He had been on my case all week to get started on it. But it's a known fact that the week you shrink for the first time and discover you have a minibrother is not the best week for getting a jump on your homework assignments.

I tried to make up for it by spending that Sunday afternoon concentrating really hard on building a great diorama. We got started and I dug right in, contributing my best ideas. For instance, I suggested we create King Tut by covering one of my Lego soldiers in shreds of toilet paper, so he looked all wrapped up like a mummy. Then we laid him down in his tomb, also known as Robin's shoe box. I thought he looked pretty Tut-ish, but Vu wasn't convinced.

"Nope," he said. "That doesn't do it. King Tut was in a coffin."

"When you're right, you're right," I said to him.

I got up and went into the bathroom, opened up the medicine cabinet, and looked through it until I found the perfect thing. A Q-tip box! I dumped the Q-tips out onto the counter and took the box to the living room.

"One coffin, at your service," I said.

"Nope," Vu said again. "King Tut's tomb was covered in gold and jewels. Not cardboard."

I went into the kitchen, opened the drawer under the silverware, got a roll of aluminum foil, and tore off a piece. It wasn't gold, but it was silver and shiny. If we wrapped the Q-tip box in it, at least you wouldn't be able to see the words "absorbent cotton-tipped swabs" on the side which, I admit, did take away from the Egyptian theme.

"Hey Robin, can I borrow a few of your rhinestones?" I asked, as long as I was there. "I need to decorate a tomb."

Without even looking up from her earring making, she shook her head no.

"Why not?" I asked.

"Because I know how you 'borrow' things," she said. "Just like you 'borrowed' my shoe box."

"Oh, you noticed."

"Well, duh. A person doesn't just toss another person's favorite pink jeweled wedgie sandals on the closet floor and not have the other person notice," she said.

I couldn't really follow the whole sandal rant, but I got the general idea that the answer was a definite no.

Fine, who needs her lousy rhinestones when you have Lola for a grandmother? Lola, the queen of weird jewelry.

Lola's room is in the back of the house, next to the sunporch where Granny Nanny lives. Lola's door was open, and I stuck my head in. She had a towel wrapped around her head. If you were paying attention before, then I don't need to tell you why. Does deep-conditioning hair day ring any bells? If it does, then welcome to my world.

"Hey Lola, can I borrow a couple of bracelets and maybe a necklace or two?"

She didn't even bat an eye. Nothing throws Lola. You could ask her for chicken-liver tea and she'd brew some up for you in a flash.

"Certainly, Daniel," she said, going to the wall where she keeps a bunch of her jewelry hanging on hooks. "Is it something to go with what you have on? I think this nice Yemeni bracelet would dress up your sweats."

"It's not for me, Lola. I need to decorate my diorama."

"Oh, how stimulating," she said. "Dioramas are such fun to make."

At last, a member of the Funk family who didn't think a diorama was some terrible tummy problem.

"How about this carved bone pendant," she said. "It was given to me on my spirit quest in Ethiopia."

"Do you have anything with a desert theme?" I asked. "We're making King Tut's tomb."

"I have the perfect thing," Lola said, taking a string of sparkling clear beads off the wall. "I got this crystal necklace from a lovely Kurdish man at a bazaar in Iran. It still smells like his camel."

"Wow, that *is* perfect," I said, taking the beads but being careful to keep them away from my nose.

Lola wanted to sing me a Kurdish folk song the camel dude had taught her, but lucky for me, I had a good excuse. I told her we were on a deadline.

"Oh yes," she said. "Mr. Stout is a stickler about promptness."

I thank you, Mr. Stout. And my ears thank you too.

"I'm glad to see you're doing such a good job on your diorama," Lola said, as she slipped her arm around my shoulder and walked me to the door. "You know I don't believe in competition. But between you and me, I'd love to see you win."

"So we can go to the All-City diorama competition?" I asked.

"No. So that Vince Bruno doesn't win. He's in my homeroom, and he keeps bragging about how he's going to win. You know I love all the world's children, but I have to make an exception for that young man. He is extremely disagreeable."

That will give you some idea of how obnoxious Vince Bruno is. I've never heard Lola say anything bad about anyone before. She always says "love is the answer." But even she couldn't get on the Pizza Prince's love train.

If I do say so myself, the aluminum foil and the crystal beads really made King Tut's tomb look slick. We built some pyramids out of Legos and covered them with a cut-up brown grocery bag so they'd be the right color. I even got some rocks from the gravel path leading to our house and glued them to the front rim of the shoe box, to show that there were boulders blocking the door to the tomb.

"It's still missing something," Vu said, when we finally took a break and inspected our work.

"Sand," I said. "King Tut's tomb was in the Valley of the Kings, which is all sand."

"Good observation," Vu said. He picked up a brown Sharpie and handed me another one. "You start on one side, I'll start on the other. We'll color the whole shoe box brown, like sand."

That sounded like a drag. Coloring the bottom of a shoe box would definitely make it onto my Top Ten list of Most Boring Things You Can Do With A Sharpie. Suddenly, an idea hit me. If you ask me, and I know you didn't, it was one of my Top Ten ideas of the month. For sure of the day.

"Vu," I said, a big smile creeping over my face. "Where do we live?"

"Venice, California," he answered.

"Yes, but what's its whole name?"

"Um . . . Venice by the Sea, California."

"Excellent. And what do you find by the sea?"

"Jellyfish. Hermit crabs. Seaweed. Starfish."

"Think beige, Vu. Think soft. Think of what gets stuck in your butt crack after you swim in the ocean."

"Sand!" he said.

"Bingo!" I shouted.

"Bingo what?"

"Bingo, we're going to put sand outside of King Tut's tomb, just like in the real Valley of the Kings. We'll go to the beach, scoop some up, scatter it around the shoebox, and finish this sucker off."

"I can't, Dan," Vu said. "I have to be at the restaurant to help my mom peel the shrimp."

Vu's parents own a Vietnamese restaurant down on Pacific Avenue near the beach. Sometimes he helps out by chopping lemon grass or stirring the soup or, in this case, peeling shrimp.

"I'll go," I said to him. "I'll bring the sand to school tomorrow and we'll pour it into the shoe box before the presentation. I bet the kids are going to think they got in a time machine and traveled to ancient Egypt."

"This is good," Vu said, nodding his head so much his gelled hair almost moved. "I'm starting to feel the win."

"And if we win, who are you inviting to the Lakers game?"

"You're in, buddy."

Vu held up his hand and we high-fived.

Oh yeah, I could already hear the basketball fans cheering.

CHAPTER 8

The Funkster's Funky Fact #8: Starfish have eight eyes, one at the end of each leg.

I put the plan into motion quickly. Even though we live only about three blocks from the beach, it's a rule that we can't go down to the sand without a grown-up. My mom and Lola were busy, and I think you and I both know doing what. (Deep-conditioning your hair takes a lot of time, friends. That's why they call it DEEP conditioning.)

But Granny Nanny agreed to go with me. She is the only grown-up female in the Funk family who has the good sense to let her hair be in whatever condition it decides it wants to be in.

I went into my room to grab my windbreaker and tell Pablo. He was sprawled out flat on my desk, his head resting on a pink rubber eraser.

"You okay?" I asked him, putting my nose right up to the desktop.

"The Pablo is fried, dude," he said. "Rock climbing has taken a toll on my perfect but tiny body."

"You stay here and rest," I said. "Granny and I are going to the beach. I'll be right back."

Pablo sat up straight as an arrow, bumping his head on the tip of my nose.

"Did you say beach?" he said. "The Pablo has recovered."

"Will Granny let you go?"

"Just take me along," he said with a grin. "We'll ask her when we get there."

I felt really bad about leaving him in my room all afternoon while I worked with Vu. I didn't want to leave him alone again. Besides, he'd be fun at the beach. We'd never been there together.

"Why not?" I said, scooping him up in my hand.

"Let's ride, Clyde," Pablo said.

"In my pocket, rocket," I answered.

Granny Nanny drives a mint-green motor scooter around town. My mom hates it when I ride on the back, but since the beach is only three blocks away, she said it was okay if we took the scooter.

I've gotten used to people staring at us when we cruise around town on Granny's scooter. I think it's her helmet with the flames on it that attracts all the attention. Or maybe people just aren't used to seeing a great-grandma on a scooter fishtailing around a corner and coming to a screeching stop in the parking lot. Which is what we did to get us to the beach in record time.

You don't have to tell me how lucky I am to live

where I live. Our beach is so cool, with a boardwalk running alongside it where people stroll and dance on Rollerblades and play paddle tennis and gather to watch the sunset every evening. Next to the boardwalk there's Muscle Beach, a stretch of Astroturf with weight-lifting equipment where guys with six-packs and big biceps work out and show off their muscles. That's Granny's favorite part of the beach.

"I'll just wait here and watch the sunset," Granny said as she parked her motor scooter in the space next to Muscle Beach.

"Granny, the sun sets over there," I said with a laugh, pointing to the ocean, which was in the opposite direction from the musclemen she was smiling at.

"A girl can look and remember when," she said softly.

I'll bet my Great Granny Nanny had some really fun boyfriends when she was young. All she'll tell me is that she looked great in a bikini and I'll have to fill in the rest myself. She did tell Pablo that she named him after her favorite two boyfriends, who were artists, which is why he's named Pablo Picasso Diego Funk.

"Okay, hotshot," Granny said with a sigh, tousling my hair and perching on the edge of a cinder-block wall. "Go get your sand and be back in five minutes. And remember what your mother says: Stay away from the storm drain."

The only bad thing about our beach is that there's a storm drain where water from the city empties into the ocean after a rain. Most days it's not a problem to go in the ocean, but my mom doesn't want us to go in the water for a couple of days after it rains. She says that storm-drain water is full of oil and antifreeze and paint and other toxic junk that people dump in the street.

So as I crossed the beach and got to the muddy water that was trickling out of the storm drain, I jumped over it.

Here's a tip: When you jump over a stream of toxic water, you should jump really far, because if you don't, you'll land right in the middle of it.

Which is what I did.

I didn't swim around in it for a long time, or go for a big splashy romp or anything. But I definitely landed in it and stayed long enough for my flip-flops to get all squishy.

I jumped out of it real fast, though, and ran to the spot on the beach where the waves met the sand. I stopped and sat down. I was planning to take off my flips and give them a rinse in the ocean while Pablo had a look around. But first I took out the plastic bag I had brought from home and scooped about four handfuls of sand into it. When I had enough to fill the diorama box, I ziplocked it shut.

I looked back to see if Granny Nanny was watching. She wasn't. Her eyes were either on Muscle Beach or the sunset. I'll let you guess which one.

I reached into my pocket, took Pablo out, and put him down on the sand.

"It's about time, dude," he said, pulling a half-eaten root beer jelly bean off his rump. "And try cleaning your pockets once in a while. The Pablo prefers to ride in a jelly bean–free zone."

I popped the rest of the jelly bean into my mouth.

I know it's gross to eat leftover pocket candy, but the truth is the truth. I ate it and actually enjoyed it. After I swallowed the jelly bean, I did giccup once or twice, but that's to be expected when you eat week-old candy.

When Pablo looked at the beach around him, I thought his eyes were going to pop out of his head! He stared at the ocean as if he had never seen anything like it before. Then suddenly it hit me. He had never seen it before!

"Is this your first time at the beach?" I asked him.

"I've been by the beach. Near the beach. Seen pictures of the beach," he said. "But I've never actually been on the beach."

"How do you like it?" I asked.

Put yourself in Pablo's place. Imagine that you're the size of the fourth toe on your left foot. Then imagine that teeny-tiny you is standing on a huge sandy beach, with ocean waves crashing in front of you and white foam nipping at your eensy-weensy toes. It would be a pretty awesome sight, right?

I'm sure it was for him. Pablo was totally blown away.

No, I mean *actually* blown away. While I was watching him watch the waves, a big gust of wind came off the ocean, picked him up off his feet, and carried him into the air.

"Pablo!" I screamed.

"Come fly with me, dude!" he yelled. "It's awesome up here."

As the wind carried him higher and higher, all I could see was the bottoms of his shoes. What if the wind kept going and lifted him so high I couldn't reach him? What if it didn't stop until he reached San Francisco? Or Alaska? Or the North Pole? What if I never saw him again?

That was completely and totally unacceptable.

I jumped up from the sand and reached out to grab him. Just as I did, the wind shifted and carried him in the opposite direction, and I found myself grabbing at air. I did a one-eighty turn, jumped as high as I could, flung my arm out and opened my hand, hoping I would catch him as he sailed above me. I missed.

"Pablo, I'm coming for you!" I called out, running through the sand.

Suddenly, my eyeballs started to growl, like the noise your stomach makes when you're really hungry.

My nose felt like it was blowing bubbles.

My fingers started to buzz.

And that whistling noise . . . was it the wind?

Or was it my knees, doing what they do before I shrink?

I won't keep you in suspense another second.

It was my knees, and yup, I was shrinking. Bamo-slamo, just like that! Down, down, down to the size of Pablo. And before I could say "Help!" or "Yikes!" or "Holy macaroni!" that same gust of wind picked me up and swept me into the air. I floated over by

Pablo, who was hovering above a shallow tide pool.

Let me tell you this: There is nothing shallow about a tide pool when you're the size of a toe. To me, it looked like Lake Titicaca. I don't even know where that is, by the way, but I'm sure it's huge.

"Check it out, bro!" Pablo called as he looked down into the tide pool. "A starfish!"

Oh, man. You haven't lived until you've seen a starfish that's two hundred times bigger than you. If you ask me, and I know you didn't, that was the creepiest creature I had ever seen.

Suddenly the wind died down, and I started to drop.

"Oh no," I hollered, "not here!"

The last thing I wanted was to be dumped on top of the prickly, spiny back of a starfish the size of a battleship.

CHAPTER 9

The Funkster's Funky Fact #9: It is impossible to tickle yourself. (Try it. It won't tickle.)

Luckily, the wind picked up again before I touched down on the starfish's back. Well, maybe it wasn't so lucky, because instead, it blew me around the beach like a feather, and I had no clue where I was going to land.

Or even if I would land at all.

Pablo was blowing around next to me, doing swimming strokes in the air, trying to battle the wind.

"This wind is getting nasty, dude," Pablo shouted, when a sudden updraft pulled him way above me. "I'm going in for a landing."

He put his hands together like he was going to dive into a pool. Then he turned himself upside down so his feet were facing the sky and his head was facing the sand. Letting out a huge martial-arts yell, the kind guys do when they break a board with their hands, Pablo kicked his feet really hard and did the breast stoke with his arms.

The wind was strong, so he didn't get very far. But he did move a little down the column of air. He yelled again, kicked again, and moved down a little more. With each yell and each kick, he came closer and closer to the sand.

Finally, he was almost down, maybe a couple inches off the sand. But when you're only an inch tall, a couple inches is still a lot.

"Now watch this, D. Funk!" he shouted to me.

He extended his arm over his head, like he was saluting the captain of an alien spaceship. Then he gave a mighty scissors kick with his feet and let out a yell that sounded like his lungs were outside his body. His body shot down like a bolt of lightning, and for one split second, he was low enough to grab the Baggie filled with sand.

He was some smart dude, my brother.

The bag of sand acted like a weight, and even though the gust of wind was still blowing hard, the weight of the sand bag anchored him down on the ground.

"Woo-hoo!" he shouted. "Now it's your turn, bro! Dive! Dive!"

I flipped over in the air and faced the sand, head down, and started paddling with my hands and feet. Either the wind was stronger or I was weaker than Pablo, because every time I got near the sand, the wind would gust and lift me up into the sky again.

This wasn't working, and I was getting really tired.

"Hang in there!" Pablo called to me.

I was trying, but to tell you the truth, I was running out of breath. I concentrated really hard, and put all my energy into the next kick. I didn't have many more in me, I could tell.

"This time, put out your hand," Pablo called to me.

I did. I kicked and paddled with all my might, and as I got close to the sand, Pablo jumped so high that even Kobe Bryant would have been proud. It was as if he had springs in his knees. He reached out to me with his right hand and grabbed onto the bag of sand with his left hand.

"I'm going to pull you in," he hollered.

The sand bag kept him firmly planted on the ground, even though the gust of wind was pulling me up. He pulled so hard, I swear I thought my little arm was going to come flying out of its little shoulder socket. I could see both his arms shaking with the strain of trying to pull me.

I held on tight to Pablo, and he held on tight to the sand bag. And finally, like one of those World War II airplanes you see on the History Channel, I came in for a beach landing.

We both lay there in the sand, clutching onto the Baggie and breathing hard.

"How fun was that," Pablo said, when he could finally talk.

"Not so much," I answered. "We could have been blown all the way to the North Pole."

"Never been there," Pablo said. "But I wouldn't mind saying 'hi' to one of those polar bears. Granny says there aren't many left, and I'm worried about them."

While I was flopped there, recovering my breath, it suddenly hit me what had just happened.

"Hey Pablo," I said to him. "You saved my life."

"No biggie. Glad to do it for you."

"But you could've been pulled back up into the air and blown away forever."

"Listen, dude," Pablo said, taking off one of his army boots and shaking the sand out of it. "You're my brother. And that means what we do, we do together. Forever, D. Funk."

I smiled. Wow, did that ever feel good.

"High-five to that," I said, putting my hand up. "Forever, P. Funk."

From a distance, I could hear Granny Nanny calling for me. Her voice sounded really far away. There was no way I could make it all the way over to her in my current body size. It would be a three-month journey, and who knows what dangers we'd run into, crossing the beach. Hermit crabs. Sand fleas. Kelp mountains. And I didn't even want to think about the soda-can tops.

"I've got to unshrink," I said to Pablo.

"By the way, what made you shrink in the first place?" he asked. "Think it was a slow-acting fish egg?"

"Maybe," I said. "Or maybe it was the seaweed. Or . . ."

While I was talking, my eyes fell on my flip-flops. They looked like they belonged to a giant. They were huge and wet and . . . wait a minute, they were wet from the storm drain water. My mom always said it was toxic.

"Or maybe it was my flip-flops," I said to Pablo.

"Whoa . . . you eating rubber now? That's sick."

"No, they got wet in the toxic water," I said. "Maybe I'm like Spider-Man, and I've had a chemical reaction, only instead of having super powers, I have shrinking powers."

That was sounding cool. I could be the star of my own comic book.

Pablo wasn't staying around to listen to my sci-fi

theory. Before I had even finished my sentence, he took off running after something on the beach.

"He's at the fifty-yard line, now the forty, now the thirty," he called.

Then he dove headfirst into the sand, as if he was diving for a loose football. And when he came up, he was holding a seagull feather.

"Got it," he said, doing a wiggle dance, like he had just scored a touchdown.

"Is that for arts and crafts?" I said.

Granny Nanny was calling even louder now. She sounded worried.

"No, it's for you, bro." With that, Pablo jumped on me and started tickling me under the nose with the bird feather. I howled with laughter. I tried to rub my nose, but he was strong and wouldn't let me get to it. It tickled. And twitched.

"Ah . . . ah . . . ah. . . ."

Ah, nothing.

"Round two," Pablo said, pouncing on me again and going after my nose with that bird feather.

"Ah . . . ah . . . ah . . . ah . . . chooooooooooooooooooooooooooooooo!"

That sneeze did it. Bamo-slamo. There I was, standing on the beach, big as life.

"Thanks, Pabs," I said. "I needed that."

I picked him up, put him in my pocket, and grabbed my bag of sand. I took off running to where Granny

LIN OLIVER

Nanny was waiting, being very careful to jump over the stream from the storm drain.

Could it have been something in that water that made me shrink? Or was it the fish eggs? Or the seaweed? Or the goulash? Or none of the above? Or all of the above?

If you ask me, and I know you didn't, this shrinking business was getting big-time confusing.

CHAPTER 10

The Funkster's Funky Fact #10: Parrots can see behind themselves without turning their heads.

Dinner at our house that night sucked even worse than usual. Not the food. The food was great. We ordered a pizza, and since the sisters insisted on getting an eggplant-and-goat-cheese pizza (I'm sorry, friends, that doesn't even deserve to be called pizza), I got a big, fat, sloppy meatball sub with extra cheese, natch. The Funk females complained that my meatball sub was unhealthy, sloppy, and gross, which was totally fine with me. That just meant I got it all.

What sucked about dinner was the conversation. Here's why:

Robin had become totally obsessed with her earrings, and you couldn't get her to shut up about them.

Lark was in heavy-duty preparation for the Women's World Poetry Festival the next day, so she decided that everything she said would be in rhyme. Yup, you heard me. In rhyme!

Goldie was still sulking about the Great Pig

Latin Insult, and therefore the only comments she'd make were about how disgusting my table manners were.

Granny Nanny had gone to bed early.

Lola was chowing down on a big bowl of *doro wat*, this Ethiopian chicken stew left over from her Global Culture Club meeting the night before. Her *doro wat* was so spicy that she had to keep rubbing an ice cube on her tongue.

My mom was totally distracted because one of her clients had brought in his parrot, Dexter, on an emergency basis that afternoon. Dexter had suddenly started to cuss a blue streak, and no one could figure out why. His owner thought maybe he had developed an anger management problem.

My mom, who's not only a vet but a certified bird nut, had brought Dexter to dinner to observe just how many swear words were coming out of his mouth. Or should I say beak?

I won't bore you with the whole dinner conversation because you would close this book and never open it again, but I feel I should give you a little sample, so you can feel my pain. Here goes:

"I think it's cool when earrings dangle all the way down to the shoulder, but Jenna and Kimberly think that mid-neck looks better."

"The table is stable. Mabel is able. There's a fable on cable."

"Eeuuww, Daniel, you're drooling mozzarella. Gross."

"Dexter, that is a very angry word. Nice birds don't talk like that."

"Oh, this *doro wat* makes my tongue sizzle!"

"Dexter! Don't make me wash your beak out with soap!"

Have you had enough? Well, I certainly had. I tell you, conversation like that will turn you into a really fast eater. Anyway, here's a tip: If you're ever invited to my house for dinner, just say no.

I ate super fast so I could get back to my room. Granny had given Pablo permission to sleep there, even though his permanent place is still in her room. She makes him the coolest little houses out of egg shells and twigs and toothpicks and stuff. Like everyone else in my family, I had always thought that Granny's tiny buildings were just sculptures, until I found out about Pablo and realized that they were really houses for him.

He and I had talked Granny into letting us move a golf-ball house she'd just finished into my room for sleepovers. We put it on the shelf next to my bed, and that's where I went looking for him when I ran into my room after dinner. I put the magnifying glass up to the little door of the hollowed-out white dome and looked inside.

"Yo, Pablo!" I called. But he wasn't in there.

Then I noticed that the PabloPhone was ringing.

Oh, it's not really a telephone. It's a device that Pablo and I made to help us communicate when I'm regular size and he's little. (I can hear him up close, but when I'm far away, I have to listen really hard for his voice.) The PabloPhone is a bunch of green plastic straws stuck together end to end. If I hold one end to my ear and he talks into the other end, his voice travels through the straw and right up into my ear. He dials me up by wiggling the straw, and since it's bright green, I usually notice.

One end of the PabloPhone was in my diorama on my desk, which I thought was kind of strange. The other end was resting on the arm of my blue La-Z-Boy chair, which is smack in the middle of my room. If you ask me, and I know you didn't, that chair is the most comfortable spot on the planet Earth. I flopped down on it, pulled the lever to the medium recline position, and put the PabloPhone up to my ear.

"Speak to me, Pabs," I said into the straw.

"What'd you bring me?" he asked. "I'm starving!"

"Meatball sandwich, extra cheese." I always try to bring Pablo a bite of something good from our dinners. You don't eat much when you're the size of a toe. One piece of popcorn lasts him a whole *Spider-Man* movie. The tiniest piece of my meatball sandwich, like the size of your thumbnail, would keep him stuffed until the next day at least.

"Do you deliver?" he said into the PabloPhone.

"I will in a few," I said. "I need to rest. It was a tough meal."

I put the PabloPhone down, hoping to just relax for a second, but it wiggled again.

"Get here now, bro."

"Are you that starving?" I asked.

"The Pablo has a surprise for you."

I happen to love surprises, so I popped myself out of the middle-recline position into the straight-up position, got out of my chair, and hurried over to the diorama on my desk.

I looked in. King Tut was lying in his tomb, like you'd expect any guy to be doing who's been dead for over two thousand years. The pyramids, the rocks, the jewels, they were all there as I'd left them. But there was something new. Another mummy had entered the scene! Propped up in front of the tomb door, holding a silver pole with a crystal bead on top, was a perfect little mummy.

A mini-mummy.

I have to admit, it added a whole new look to the diorama. I mean, one mummy is good, but two mummies are twice as good. Or as Lark would say when she's in her rhyming mood, *twice as nice.*

At first I thought it was a small Lego guy that Pablo had found and wrapped in toilet paper. But when the mini-mummy turned to look at me and wiggled his rump in a familiar dance, I realized this was no Lego guy. This was Pablo!

"Is that you in there?" I asked, practically sticking my nose in his mummified face.

"It's amazing what a little toilet paper can do," he said, talking through a slit he had made in the toilet paper near his mouth. I noticed he had also left his feet unwrapped, which is how he was managing to wiggle the PabloPhone.

"Who are you supposed to be?" I asked.

"One of King Tut's servants. You know, those Egyptian GUPS buried servants in their tombs with them, to serve them food and stuff in the afterlife."

I had actually read that in my history book . . . not the GUP part, but the rest of it. I had to hand it to Pablo. He had learned a lot about ancient Egypt.

"Well, you look very cool," I said. "Nice job on the T.P."

"Shredded it myself."

"And what's this?" I asked, pointing to the silver pole.

"Adds a nice touch, don't you think?"

"Yeah, it makes you look official."

"I made it myself by wrapping a Q-tip in tin foil. One of the sisters left a whole pile of them in the bathroom. And they say us guys are messy."

I didn't have the heart to tell him that it was me who was the Q-tip slob.

"So am I going?" Pablo asked.

"Going where?"

"To school with you. I want to be in the diorama."

"No way, Pablo. That's crazy."

Pablo started to jump up and down, which loosened

the toilet paper shreds around his legs and arms.

"I object," he said, as he peeled off the rest of the toilet paper.

"Listen, Pablo. You can't just hang out in the world like you're normal size," I said to him. "Look what happened at the beach today."

"What happened at the beach is that *I* saved *your* life!" he said.

"It was dangerous for you."

"Let me point out, bro, that *you* were the one in danger. Not *me*."

He was kind of yelling. Wow. This was our first fight. It was very different from fighting with my sisters. They just whine and stomp their feet and then cry and get their way. Pablo and I were disagreeing, but we were actually talking.

"Granny won't let you go," I said.

"We don't have to tell her until I'm there. Then we'll call and let her know everything's okay."

"Pablo, I'm responsible for you."

"No you're not! I'm the older brother, dude. Remember?"

"By thirty seconds, maybe."

"Thirty seconds is thirty seconds."

"I have to think this over," I said. "Give me a minute."

I flopped down in my La-Z-Boy, which is where I do my best thinking.

First I thought of all the dangers of bringing Pablo to school and hiding him in the diorama. He could fall out. Someone could steal him. He could sneeze and blow off his toilet paper, and then everyone would see him as a real boy and not a mummy. That would reveal our secret forever.

On the other hand, I thought about how much he wanted to come with me. I thought of how interested he was in ancient Egypt. I thought of how cool he looked in his mummy gear, and how he wanted to be a part of the diorama. I thought of how long I had waited to share my life and my fun times with a brother, and of how happy he would be for me if we won.

"You guys are a team," a little voice inside me said. "The Funk Brothers. Daniel and Pablo. Pablo and Daniel. Together. Forever."

I got out of my chair and walked over to the diorama. Pablo was pacing back and forth on the desk. He looked mad. And I didn't blame him.

"Pabs?" I said.

"Bro?" he said.

"Get out the toilet paper," I said. "You're coming with me."

CHAPTER 11

The Funkster's Funky Fact #11: Early Hawaiians used coconut shells for toilet paper.

In the morning, we rewrapped Pablo in his mummy costume, using new toilet paper, of course. If you ask me, and I know you didn't, I think it's a bad idea to use toilet paper twice.

I put Pablo in the back corner of the diorama shoe box, but he made me promise to let him move to the front during the actual presentation. I was nervous showing him to my mom at breakfast. It was a test to see if he'd pass as a real mummy. I mean a real fake mummy.

"Very nice, honey," was all my mom said when I showed her the diorama.

I guess that meant Pablo passed.

It wasn't a true test, though, because my mom wasn't really concentrating. She was all in a twist because Lark was all in a twist. It seems the Big Sis had broken a string on her lap harp as she was loading it into the car. I tried to tell her that this was good news because it was one less string that was going to sound awful. Let me put it this way: She wasn't amused.

I couldn't believe my mom was actually taking off a whole day of work to accompany Lark to the Women's World Poetry Festival. I mean, she didn't come when I made it to the quarter-finals of the Venice Beach Indoor Remote-Control Car Thunder Derby. Of course, that day she was operating on a king snake who had mistaken a Porsche Matchbox car for a mouse and swallowed it. I remember that she felt so bad about missing my event that she let me keep the toy Porsche. I still have it.

After Lark and my mom left, Lola drove Robin and me to our school, the Ocean Avenue Middle School. Even though she's a teacher there, Lola usually doesn't drive me in the morning because she has to be there extra early, and personally, I like to sleep extra late. But since Robin had to be there early to set up her earring stand, and I didn't want to carry the diorama, we all went together.

A bunch of Robin's volleyball friends were waiting for her in the parking lot. They had little plastic bags with earrings in them too. They were all totally amped up about their earring sale. I'm telling you, with all the squealing and squeaking that was going on, they should have been selling earplugs instead.

As I got out of Lola's car, I balanced the diorama in one hand and my backpack, lunch, and the sand-

filled Baggie in the other. I was doing a pretty good job, making my way up the ramp to the Anchorage Building, where my locker is. All the buildings at our school have oceany-boaty kinds of names like Catamaran or Topsail or Jib or Hurricane. The plan was to put my other stuff in my locker, then hold on to the diorama with two hands until I met Vu. I wasn't taking any chances of losing Pablo.

When I reached the double-glass door to

Anchorage, I ran into a little problem. The door was closed, and if I wanted to open it, I was one hand short. I tried to lift the door handle with my knee, but I couldn't get my leg up that high.

"Let me help you with that," a voice said.

I turned around to see Vince Bruno grabbing the door handle for me. Vince isn't the kind of person who's known for holding doors for people in need. He's not what you'd call a helpful kind of guy. He's more what you'd call a total "me" person. He thinks he's better than everyone because his parents are rich from the chain of Pizza Kings they own. He gets everything he wants. He even gets stuff he doesn't even want. All he does is brag nonstop because he has the best skateboard, the best cell phone, the best laptop, the best iPod, the best sneakers, blah blah blah blah blah.

If you ask me, and I know you didn't, what Vince Bruno definitely doesn't have is the best personality.

Not to be rude, but the guy is a major-league jerk.

"Thanks, Vince," I said, slipping through the door as he held it open for me. He might be a jerk, but manners are manners.

"You can call me the Pizza Prince," he said.

Oh yeah, like I'm going to do that.

"Maybe another time, dude. For now, I'll just stick with 'Vince.'"

The Pizza Prince actually wasn't a bad name for him. He looked kind of like a pizza. His face was round and red and well . . . if I were being polite, I would say blotchy. But if I weren't being so polite, I'd say zitty. He had bright red hair, buzzed short, which made his whole head looked like a ripe red tomato. His body was round like a pizza too. Not fat. The guy's a wrestler, after all. But he was solid and pale and round, like the human version of a mound of pizza dough.

Why was the Pizza Prince walking down the hall next to me? It wasn't like he was a friend or anything.

"Bye, Vince," I said, which I thought was a subtle way of telling him to disappear. I had better things to do than deal with him. I was hoping Vu and I had time to do a final run-through of our presentation. Mr. Stout's history class was first period, which was coming right up.

But Vince stuck right next to me, like pepperoni on a cheese pizza.

"Excuse me, Double P," I said to him, "but I'm in kind of a hurry here."

I tried to walk past him to my locker, but he caught up with me.

"Hey, let me see your diorama," he said. "What'd you do it on?"

"King Tut."

"You and everybody else," he said with a snicker. I told you the guy's a jerk.

"Mine's on the invention of pizza," he said. "Bet you a hundred dollars no one else is doing that."

"You win, Vince. Go buy yourself a couple of pizzas."

Oh no. What was that sound? It was laughter coming from inside my shoe box.

I think we both know who it was.

"Nice comeback, bro," Pablo called out. He must have been really shouting because I could hear him and even make out the words.

"What'd you say, Funk?" Vince asked, in not such a friendly tone of voice.

"I didn't say anything. It was just my stomach growling. Must've been all that pizza talk got me hungry."

I made a growling sound with my mouth, to emphasize the point.

"Wait until you see my diorama," Mr. Tomato Head went on. "I'm going to win for sure."

This guy was totally getting on my nerves.

"It's a multisensory experience," Vince said. "You can see it, smell it, and taste it."

"What's it made of, pizza dough?" I said, laughing.

"As of matter of fact, it is. I rubbed garlic on the

inside of the box, wrapped the whole thing in dough and baked it my dad's pizza oven. I'm sure you probably know, but in case I didn't mention it, my dad owns Pizza King."

"Really?" I said. "I didn't know that."

Another hoot came from inside my shoe box.

"He shoots, he scores!" I heard Pablo say.

Vince gave me a funny look and I repeated what Pablo said, making that mouth growling sound again as I talked.

"Man, you are one strange guy," Vince said. "I never noticed that before."

"So, where is this great diorama of yours?" I asked.

"I already dropped it off in Mr. Stout's room," he said. "It's just sitting there, waiting to win first place."

"Wait until Mr. Garlic meets King Tut," I said. "You might be surprised."

I'm not 100 percent sure about what happened next, but I'm 99 percent sure.

I think the big jerk stuck his expensive super-trendy cross-trainer out in front of me and tripped me. On purpose. I don't mean to brag, but I'm a pretty good athlete, and it's a known fact that pretty good athletes don't just go around tripping on their own feet for no reason.

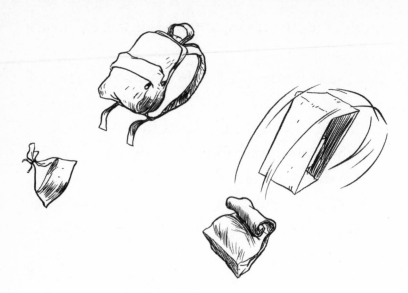

Man, did I go flying. My backpack went up, my lunch went down, and the sand bag went sideways. Worst of all, the diorama left my hands and went sailing forward, flying like a Frisbee through the air.

As I watched it, everything went kaflooey in my head. It was as if the world shifted into slow motion.

I heard Vince Bruno's laugh, loud and echo-y in my ears.

I saw the silver shoe box turn over and over in the air.

I caught a glimpse of Pablo, clutching on to one of the Lego pyramids.

I watched the smelly camel-dude's necklace wrap itself around and around the diorama, making a

LIN OLIVER

tinkling sound as the crystal beads clinked against one another.

Our diorama was sinking.

The whole thing, all our work and creativity, was falling down, down, down to the concrete floor.

Oh no. Oh no. Oh no.

If there is an Angel of Flying Dioramas, and I believe there is, I hoped that she would protect me now.

CHAPTER 12

The Funkster's Funky Fact #12: In ancient Egypt, the average man was only about five feet tall.

All my years of playing baseball paid off in that one second.

I sprang into the air like I was reaching to catch a pop fly. I stretched so far to the right that my arm felt like it had doubled in length. And then I dove, both legs off the ground, attempting the most difficult diving catch of my life.

And guess what?

The Angel of Flying Dioramas was watching over me, because I caught that shoe box just before it splatted onto the concrete floor.

When I looked up, I saw Vince Bruno running down the hall as fast as he could, like the cowardly tomato-head bully he is.

"You okay in there?" I asked Pablo, as I checked out the inside of the diorama.

"Let me at that jerk," was all he said. "I'm going to wipe the floor with him."

"Pablo, he'd step on you and squash you like a flea."

"Well, he's not going to get away with this," he

said, pacing back and forth like he does when he's really mad.

"Hey, stop that pacing," I said to him. "Your toilet paper is going to unravel."

By the time we got to Mr. Stout's room, Pablo had calmed down somewhat. I could see Vu waiting anxiously outside the door for me. I knew it meant a lot to him to get into the All-City competition. Me, I mainly wanted the Lakers tickets. But Vu didn't want to disappoint his parents. They really want Vu to do well in school so he can go to college and make them proud.

"There's Vu," I whispered to Pablo. "You ready?"

"I'm ready to pop the Pizza Prince in the nose."

"Let it go, Pablo. Concentrate. Get into your position by the front of the tomb. Stand still."

"Okay, I'll drop it for now," he said. "I am your servant mummy."

"Promise?"

"You have The Pablo's word."

He put his silver pole by his side, placed one hand on King Tut's coffin, and stood completely still, staring into space. I have to confess, he looked fantastic.

"Everything okay?" Vu said, as I walked up to the classroom door. "You're late."

"Yeah, I had a little trip down the hall," I said.

"Vince the Pizza Prince got his big foot stuck in front of my leg."

"He's inside already," Vu said, "telling everyone how he's got the win in the bag."

"We'll beat him," I reassured Vu. "I have a surprise that will cinch the deal. I added a mini-mummy last night."

Vu looked inside the diorama and stared at Pablo. I held my breath, hoping that Pablo would stay still, like he was supposed to.

"Wow," said Vu. "He looks so real."

I couldn't change the topic fast enough.

"Here's the sand from the beach," I said, waving the Baggie in front of Vu to distract him. "We'll pour it out just before we do the presentation, so none of it spills."

We carried our diorama into class and set it down on the side counter with the others. There were thirteen in all. Everyone worked in teams of two. Everyone but Vince, that is. He had refused to team up with anyone.

"I'm the star of my own team," he had told Mr. Stout. "Why have a partner who will only bring you down?"

After the bell rang, we drew numbers from a hat to see who would go first. Vu and I drew number twelve, which meant we were going next to last. That worried me, because Pablo was going to have to stay still for almost the whole period. I got the idea to cover our diorama with my jacket. That way, Pablo could relax during the other presentations and not have to worry about keeping still.

The Pizza Prince drew number thirteen.

"We'll save the best for last," he said. Mr. Stout told him to take his seat and zip his lip.

The first three presentations were all girls, and every one of their dioramas was the same—the Pilgrims landing at Plymouth Rock. What is it with girls and Pilgrims, anyway? Finally, Alan Baker and Marcus Kendall-Waxman presented an interesting one, showing how the dinosaurs got stuck in tar and became extinct. It was cool because they made the tar out of lots of already-been-chewed gum. One of those guys must have liked bubble gum, because I had never seen pink tar before.

When it was finally our time to present, I got the diorama and carried it to the front of the room. I kept my jacket over it.

"It's showtime," I whispered to Pablo. "Don't mess up."

"You talking to your jacket, Funk?" Vince called out. "That's weird."

"I'm just rehearsing my lines," I explained to Mr. Stout. He nodded at me and told Vince to zip his lip again.

When I removed my jacket, a couple of kids in the front row actually applauded. Our scene really did look great, especially Pablo. He had moved up to the front of the shoe box and was kneeling down by King Tut's coffin.

"He wasn't kneeling before," Vu whispered. "How'd you do that?"

"I'm a Lego master," I said. "You be the sand master."

Vu opened the bag of beach sand and poured it over the whole bottom of the diorama. Man, it looked so real. Actually, why wouldn't it look real? It *was* real.

Vu stood on one side of our diorama and I stood on the other.

"Welcome to ancient Egypt," I began. "Land of pyramids and pharaohs."

I paused and waited for Vu to chime in, as we had rehearsed. He didn't say anything, just stared at his feet. He was really nervous. Finally, he spoke.

"Back in the day, there lived a boy king named Tutankhamen," he said, but somewhere between the Tut and the Khamen, his voice cracked really badly.

LIN OLIVER

It sounded like he had a rubber horn in his throat.

"Sounds like somebody swallowed a frog," Vince whispered, loud enough so everyone could hear. Even though Mr. Stout told him to zip his lip and keep it zipped this time, some kids in the class laughed.

All right, I was going to get their attention back. I could do this.

"King Tut died at only sixteen years of age," I said in my best public speaking voice, "and was buried in a hidden tomb that looked exactly like this one."

With a flourish, I waved my hand in front of our diorama. That seemed to relax Vu, and he waved his hand too. Then he smiled and went on with his speech. This was starting to go really well. We were rock stars.

"King Tut's tomb was forgotten until 1922," he said, "when it was discovered by an Englishman named Howard Carter. If you listen, you can hear him now."

"Oowwww!" screamed a small voice. "Get off my rear end!"

Vu snapped his head around and stared at me.

"What's wrong with you?" he whispered. "You're not supposed to say that!"

It wasn't me, of course. It was Pablo. But why was he screaming? And who was on his rump?

Here's a tip: If you're ever giving an oral report, and your diorama suddenly starts talking, pretend it didn't happen.

That's what I did.

"Not only was Tut's tomb filled with golden treasure, it also contained his mummy," I said, speaking loudly enough to drown out Pablo if he felt the urge to speak up again.

Naturally, he did.

"Hey! You're ripping my toilet paper!" he shouted.

There was no ignoring him this time. I knew the

kids in class couldn't hear him, but I thought Vu could.

"Stop fooling around, Dan," he whispered. "This matters to me."

I had to put an end to this. I grabbed my jacket from the table and threw it over the diorama.

"Time out," I said to the class. "The mummies are restless and would like a word with me."

I couldn't tell if Vu was angry or confused. I can tell you this, he didn't look happy.

The last thing I heard as I stuck my head under my jacket was Vince's loud laugh.

"This is priceless!" he said.

I hope you're sitting down, because you're not going to believe what I saw in our shoe box. A sand crab about as big as Pablo had attached itself to his behind and was shredding his mummy costume with its crabby claws.

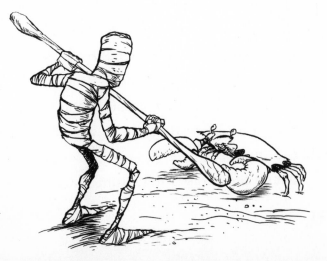

"Way to check out the sand, bro," Pablo said, swatting at the crab with his silver Q-tip. "Down, big fella."

"Ssshhh," I whispered.

"Easy for you to say, dude. You don't have this guy munching on your rump."

I reached in and pulled the sand crab off Pablo's body.

"Much better," Pablo said. "I hope there's no more where he came from."

"Now kneel down," I whispered. "And hurry."

Pablo assumed his position by the mummy's coffin, keeping his rear end to the back wall of the tomb so that you couldn't see his behind poking out of the shredded toilet paper. When he was settled, I removed the jacket and turned back to the class.

"Is everything okay, Daniel?" Mr. Stout asked.

"I've made a lucky find," I said, holding up the little sand crab for everyone to see.

"What are you doing, Dan?" Vu whispered.

"Watch and learn," I whispered back.

"Behold what I've discovered in King Tut's tomb—this ancient scarab, the magical beetle charm used by the Egyptians to ward off evil and bring good luck into the afterlife."

"That's a sand crab, you moron," Vince called out.

"Only to those with no imagination," I answered. "If you close your eyes, you can feel the presence of King Tut in the spirit of this prized ancient scarab."

Everyone closed their eyes but Mr. Stout. He picked up his pencil and wrote something down in his roll book.

I wondered what it was.

CHAPTER 13

The Funkster's Funky Fact #13: There is an actual sport called toe-wrestling. The championship tournament is held in England every year.

I'm not going to keep you wondering. I like you too much to do that.

Mr. Stout wrote, "Excellent presentation. Original ideas. Definitely a finalist."

Pretty cool, huh?

Unfortunately, the other finalist was none other than Vince The Pizza Prince, with his multisensory scene of the invention of pizza. Since only one diorama could be selected to go to All-City, we were going to have to go toe-to-toe with the big twit at the assembly after lunch. The students were going to pick the winner.

Ladies and Gentlemen.

In the center ring, Daniel Funk and Vu Tran take on Vince Bruno.

The mini-mummy versus the garlic pizza monster.

Man, this was going to be some fight.

CHAPTER 14

The Funkster's Funky Fact #14: The first portable cell phone, made in 1973, was the size of a brick.

"We almost won!" I shouted to Robin, running up to the table where she and her girl pals were selling earrings.

"Almost? What's so great about that? That's like *almost* getting asked to the prom. Or *almost* getting chosen MVP of the volleyball team. Or *almost* eating an ice cream sundae. Or—"

"I get the point, Robs. Anyway, you've got to ask all your friends to come to the assembly and vote for us."

"Fat chance, Daniel," she said. "As if my friends are interested in your little sixth-grade projects."

"I'm interested," her friend Hailey said.

"Me too," Jenna said.

"Me three," said Kimberly.

"Great, we'll be there," Robin said. "Wouldn't miss it."

I don't know why girls have to make decisions in groups of at least four. Guys don't do that. Either you want to go to the assembly and you go, or you don't and you don't go. Maybe it takes four girl brains to equal one guy brain. Wait, I take that back. It was mean.

True, but mean.

"Oh, by the way," Robin said, as I was walking away. "Granny Nanny left the weirdest message on my phone. She said to tell you she can't find the little one and you have to call her right away."

Oops. In all the excitement of being a finalist, I had forgotten to call Granny and tell her that Pablo was with me.

"What little one?" Jenna asked.

I noticed everyone was waiting for an answer.

"Oh, the little one. Yeah . . . um . . . I think she couldn't find her little . . . um . . . pencil," I said. "Granny gets upset when she can't find a little pencil because she's a little woman with little hands, and big pencils are just so big and heavy and not little."

The girls just stared at me.

"Could you not be such a goofball?" Robin whispered.

"I was just answering the question."

"Yeah, weirdly."

"Listen, Robs, I need to borrow your phone so I can call Granny."

"Dream on."

We're not allowed to have cell phones in school. Well, we're allowed to *have* them, we're just not allowed to *use* them, which is a rule I've never understood. Why have a cell phone if you're not going to use it? Robin always has hers, though, because it's permanently attached to her body and she can't be separated from it without having major surgery.

"Fine, Robin. Just let Granny stay all worried then."

"Okay, okay," she said with a sigh, handing me her phone. "Try not to spit on it when you talk. And do not let anyone see you using it."

That wasn't going to be easy. It was lunchtime and everyone was wandering around campus. I needed privacy, and the most private place I could think of was the boys' bathroom in the Anchorage Building. I ran down there, went into a stall, locked the door, got out the phone, and speed-dialed home.

Okay, friends. I confess. I should have looked under the next stall and checked for feet, but I didn't. If I had, I would have seen a pair of cross trainers—a very *expensive* pair of cross-trainers—attached to a pair of beefy pizza legs.

Go ahead. Tell me I'm stupid. It's not like my sisters don't tell me all the time. You're right. I admit it. I was stupid for not noticing that Vince Bruno was in the stall next to me.

Granny answered the phone right away, almost before it rang.

"Daniel, I can't find Pablo!" she said.

"He's with me," I answered.

"Where?"

"In my pocket."

That was true. He was so pooped after his diorama performance and his battle with the sand crab, I had to put him in my shirt pocket for a nap.

"Tell her I'm fine," he said sleepily from inside my shirt.

"I would if I could get a word in," I whispered to him. "She's mad and says she's coming to get you."

"Let me talk to her."

"Okay, but make it quick."

I thought I heard something in the stall next to me. It wasn't a toilet flushing and it wasn't regular footsteps. It was something that sounded like a shuffling noise, as if someone were walking really really fast on their tiptoes. It suddenly occurred to me to check for feet in the stall next to me. I know, I know. I was late in having that thought. What do you want from me? I've already apologized.

I checked under the stall to see if any feet were there. Nope, none. So I reached into my pocket and

gave Pablo a boost up. I held the phone right next to my left pec so he could talk into it. The phone, not the pec, that is.

"Hey, Gran-apple," he said. "How's tricks, you kind, lovely, wonderful lady you? No, I am not sweet-talking you. Yeah, I know I should've asked. But hey, you always say you want me to get an education, and here I am in school."

Granny went on talking, but Pablo was done listening. He yawned and dropped back down into my shirt pocket.

"Wake me when it's over," he said.

I put the phone back up to my ear, and Granny

talked a mile a minute, going on and on about how this wasn't a responsible decision. She was right in the middle of listing all the scary thoughts she had when she couldn't find him, when I heard footsteps in the bathroom. Then a voice.

"Daniel?" it said. "Come out of there right now."

It was Principal Dirk Quirk, head of our middle school, a tall, thin man with a long, thin face and bushy black eyebrows.

"Got to go," I whispered to Granny and clicked the phone shut.

"Hi, Mr. Quirk," I said as I shoved the phone in my jeans pocket and opened the stall door.

Standing next to Mr. Quirk was none other than . . . you guessed it . . . Vince Bruno. That tomato head had walked himself and his stupid expensive cross-trainers down to Mr. Quirk's office and ratted on me.

"Are you talking on a cell phone, Daniel?" Mr. Quirk asked.

Now, I am capable of doing a lot of bad things, but looking right in the face of the school principal and telling a flat-out lie is not one of them.

"I made a call, but it was an emergency."

"That's why we have phones in the office," Mr. Quirk said. "Give me the cell, Daniel. You can get it back at the end of the week."

Robin was going to kill me. I was a goner. Dead meat. Brother stew.

I handed the phone to Mr. Quirk.

"Hot pink," the Pizza Prince said with a laugh. "Nice choice of color, Funk."

"Thank you for your help, Vincent," Mr. Quirk said, "but don't you have someplace to be now?"

"Sure do," Vince said. "I have to present my diorama in a few minutes at the assembly."

"Me too," I said, starting to leave.

"Not so fast, Daniel," Mr. Quirk said. "I'd like you to come with me to the office."

"Why? All I did was make one little call!"

"Vincent here tells me that you were acting strangely," Mr. Quirk said. "Talking to someone who wasn't there, as if there were another person in the stall with you. I think we should discuss this."

"I've got to go. I have to be in the auditorium in ten minutes. I'm fine, Mr. Quirk, really."

"Talking to someone who isn't there is not fine, Daniel."

"And he was doing the other guy's voice, too," Vince chimed in. "This little teeny voice that sounded like it came from a miniature person. It was really weird."

Wow, Vince must have had his ear pressed up to the stall to be able to hear Pablo. I tried to come up with a way to explain the fact that he heard Pablo's voice. But I blurted out exactly the wrong thing.

"I was practicing having a conversation," I said. "Because I'm shy and sometimes I just like to practice talking. So I have an imaginary friend I talk to. He's got a little voice because he's a little imaginary friend."

Oh boy. That really didn't sit well with Mr. Quirk. I saw him raise one of his bushy black eyebrows and give me a strange look.

"Imaginary friends are fine in preschool, but not in middle school," Mr. Quirk said. "I think we need to discuss this habit of yours with your mother."

"You can't. She's at a poetry festival."

Oh yeah! I love you, Lark Sparrow Funk. I love your geeky poetry festival and your lap harp and that you took Mom away for the whole day.

Mr. Quirk took Robin's pink cell phone out of his pocket, and pressed a button. I could see her contact list come up on the screen. Just my luck, to have a principal who knows how to speed dial.

"Ah, I see your mother's number right here. Let's just try her, shall we?" he said.

Before I could answer, he had my mom's number on the phone. When she answered, he told her there was a matter that had come up at school that needed her immediate attention. He asked her to come to school right away.

"She'll be here as soon as she can," Mr. Quick said.

About the love thing, Lark. I take it back. Especially the part about the lap harp.

"Mr. Quirk, can't I please go?"

"Not until I've discussed this with your family. Until then, you're staying in my office."

No! This wasn't happening!

"But the diorama competition—"

"Don't feel bad, buddy," Vince said. "You wouldn't have won anyway."

His round zitty face was all pink and happy, like a sausage pizza with red peppers.

It made me never want to eat pizza again.

CHAPTER 15

The Funkster's Funky Fact #15: In North America, cinnamon is the second most often used flavoring, after pepper.

I sat in Mr. Quirk's office, watching the minutes tick by on the big clock on his wall. I wasn't even wondering if I was in trouble or what I would say when my mom got there. I just kept thinking about Vu, how nervous he would be without me there, and how much he would probably mess up. Then we would lose, the Pizza Prince would win, and two perfectly good seats to a Lakers game would disappear forever.

By the way, did I mention that I've never been to a Lakers game in my life? And that I'm a huge fan?

Well, it didn't seem to matter, because in another three minutes, lunch would be over, the assembly would begin, and I could kiss the most fun night of my life good-bye.

"Do you feel like talking, Daniel?" Mr. Quirk asked, staring at me from under his bushy eyebrows.

"Only if we can talk about me going to the assembly."

Mr. Quirk looked irritated. He reached up with one hand and twirled his eyebrow hair. No kidding. His eyebrows were so bushy they were actually twirlable.

"I've explained to you, Daniel, that I need to keep you here until I've spoken with your family. Your mother should arrive shortly."

How could I tell this guy that shortly was too late?

Then it hit me. Lola! He said he wanted to talk with my family. She was my family, and she was right there at school.

"Mr. Quirk, why don't you go get my grandmother?" I said. "She's family, and she'll tell you I'm fine."

"Daniel, that's an excellent suggestion. You wait right here, and I'll be back with your grandmother. Ms. Donovan will keep an eye on you."

Holy macaroni, I couldn't believe he said that.

Ms. Donovan is Principal Quirk's assistant, who sits in the office out front. Everyone knows that she only has one eye. The other one is glass. And he said she'll keep *an eye* on you. You'd think in principal school they'd teach you how to be more sensitive.

Mr. Quirk wasn't gone two seconds when Pablo popped his head out of my pocket.

"Please tell me we're not going to miss the assembly, bro."

"You heard Mr. Quirk. He said to stay here."

"And since when do we have to listen to that big GUP?"

"Since always, Pablo. He's the principal. Besides, Ms. Donovan is watching."

"So we escape, dude. Fly low. Under the radar."

"Right, and how do you suggest we do that?"

"It's simple, dimple. You shrink."

"Just like that? No goulash. No fish egg. No seaweed. No toxic water."

"Dude," Pablo said, crawling up my shirt and perching on my shoulder so I could hear him really well. "You don't even know that those are the things that make you shrink. Maybe it's all in your mind, and if you concentrate hard enough, you can shrink yourself. Maybe that's what you've been doing all along."

I looked up and noticed that Ms. Donovan was watching me. Oh, great. Now she could be another person telling Mr. Quirk that I was talking to myself.

Here's a tip: When a grown-up is giving you a look, you know, the "what's-that-kid-think-he's-doing" kind of look, flash them a big smile and then finish it off with a wave. I call it my smiley-wave, and I tell you, it just melts their GUP hearts.

I smiled at Ms. Donovan, and gave her a nice wave. She reached into her desk drawer, stood up, and walked toward me.

"GUP alert," I whispered to Pablo. "Under the collar, quick."

I usually just wear T-shirts, but I had dressed up for the diorama presentation, so luckily I had a collar he could duck under. I turned sideways so the part of my collar that Pablo was hiding under was facing Ms. Donovan's glass eye. Sorry if this sounds rude. I have absolutely nothing against people with glass eyes. I just thought you needed to know, that's all.

"Would you like a cinnamon drop, Daniel?" Ms. Donovan said.

"That's very nice of you, Ms. Donovan."

She handed me a red candy in a clear wrapper and smiled. I unwrapped the candy, put it in my mouth, and smiled back at her. Then she left. What'd I tell you about the smiley-wave. Works every time.

"All clear," I whispered to Pablo, after she had gone back to her desk.

"Okay, no time to lose," he said. "Close your eyes and concentrate on what I'm saying. Let yourself see everything I say."

"Whoa, this cinnamon drop is spicy," I said. "Makes me giccup."

"Dude, that is so not concentrating."

I closed my eyes, stifled another giccup, and tried to block out everything but Pablo's voice.

"I feel myself getting smaller," he said, scrunching right up next to me, so he was almost in my ear. It felt like that time a fly flew in my ear at summer camp. "My hands are getting smaller. My feet are getting smaller. Even my nostrils are getting smaller."

I was trying to see everything he said, but that nostril thing was hard. I don't spend a lot of time visualizing my nostrils. Sometimes I think about my nose, but never the holes inside it. I was so busy trying to get my head into what a shrinking nostril looks like that I didn't even notice the sound at first.

Could it be? Yes, it could.

My eyeballs were definitely growling.

My nostrils (not my nose) felt like they were blowing bubbles.

The buzzing in my fingers got so loud, I was worried Ms. Donovan would hear. And just as my knees started to whistle, bamo-slamo, I shrunk. It was so fast and sudden that the cinnamon drop came flying out of my mouth. It's a known fact that you can't keep something in your mouth that is bigger than your mouth itself.

"It worked," I said to Pablo. "I did it. I shrunk myself. Unless maybe it was the cinnamon candy."

"No time for this," Pablo said.

"Granny did mention once that she puts cinnamon in her goulash."

"Yo dude, save it. We have to get to the auditorium. Let's jet, Brett."

"It's all the way across campus. We'll never make it."

I heard Mr. Quirk's footsteps coming into the office.

"Your grandmother wasn't in her classroom, Daniel," he was saying. "Daniel? Daniel? Ms. Donovan, where did Daniel go?"

"I don't know, sir," she said, peeking into his office with a confused look on her face. "He was just here a minute ago."

"He must have snuck out," Mr. Quirk said. "This is unacceptable."

He reached up and started knitting his eyebrow. It was so long, he could have made a sweater.

"Shall I go look for him, sir?" Ms. Donovan said.

"No, I'll go find him. I imagine he's gone to the auditorium."

"Come on! Now's our chance!" Pablo whispered.

"To do what?"

"To catch a lift. The Pablo says, why walk when you can ride?"

Pablo grabbed my hand and pulled me to the edge of the chair. I looked down. All I could see

was Mr. Quirk's shoes. They were brown loafers with a tassel on top.

"Jump!" Pablo said. "Aim for the tassel. It will break the fall."

"It's a long way down there. You can't hit that."

"Oh yeah? Remember Pablo's Drop Zone?"

"You mean your rock-climbing crash pad."

"Right. I've never missed it."

"But I saw you miss it."

"Well, maybe once I did. Or twice. Three times, tops. The point is, bro, we have no choice now. Let's go! Three, two, one, blast-off!"

He gave a tug on my hand and we jumped. To be more specific, Pablo jumped and I just sort of followed. Whoa. It seemed like we were falling forever.

If you ask me, and I know you didn't, my brother has an amazing aim. We landed smack-dab in the middle of the tassel.

"Bull's-eye!" Pablo said, grabbing on to the fluffy leather tassel with one hand and pumping his fist with the other.

"Thank you, Pablo's Drop Zone," I said. "Man, am I glad you practiced that jump!"

"Who said I practiced? I've never jumped from that height before in my life."

Can you believe the guts that guy has?

Suddenly the shoe lifted off the ground, and I grabbed hold of the tassel fast. Boy, when Mr. Quirk walks, he really walks. He was like one of those speed walkers in the Olympics. Without the tassel to hold on to, we would have been thrown off like cowboys on a bucking bronco.

I was getting a little motion sickness from all the loafer action. But not Pablo. He just kicked back and enjoyed the view of the other feet as they hurried down the hall.

"Think we'll make it in time for the presentation?" I asked.

"You got bigger questions to ask, bro."

He was right. Like, could I unshrink myself when we got there? And how would I explain my sudden disappearance to Mr. Quirk? And would my mom think I was crazy?

And most important, where were we going to get a roll of fresh toilet paper? A mummy has to look his best, you know.

CHAPTER 16

The Funkster's Funky Fact #16: In Thailand, it is considered an extreme insult for shoes or feet to touch someone else's head.

Mr. Quirk made it to the auditorium in record time, and since we were riding on his shoe, so did we. Wow, the room was buzzing with kids. They had turned out big-time for the diorama competition. Or maybe it was for the free cookies and lemonade the parents association was serving.

"Has anyone seen Daniel Funk?" I heard Mr. Quirk say.

"I'm looking for him too," Robin said. "The little creep swiped my cell phone."

"You won't be seeing that for a while, young lady," he said. "I'm keeping it until the end of the school week."

"You're not!" Robin said.

"I am!" he answered.

"I'll die!" she said.

"You won't!" he answered. "People have been known to survive for three days without a cell phone."

Oh yeah? He doesn't know my sister Robin. Last

time she couldn't find her cell phone, Lola had to make her a whole pot of organic Nighty-Night tea and put her to bed.

"I need to find Daniel too," said a voice that sounded just like Granny Nanny's. That's because it was Granny Nanny. When did she arrive?

"And who are you?" Principal Quirk asked her.

"I'm his great-grandmother."

"Oh, the lady who likes little pencils," Robin's friend Jenna said. "That's so cute."

Before Granny could say, "What in the world are you talking about, kid?" Lola showed up.

"Dirk," she said. "I was in the teacher's lounge and I heard you were looking for me."

"His name is Dirk Quirk?" Granny Nanny said. "Now that's a crying shame."

I had always thought that Mr. Quirk's name was what had turned him into such a sourpuss. I mean, how would you like to go through life with eyebrows so long you could knit a sweater out of them *and* have a name like Dirk Quirk. Elementary school must have been a total nightmare for him.

"I'm glad you're here, Lola," Mr. Quirk said. "We have a little situation with your grandson."

"What seems to be the problem?" Wait a minute—that was my mom's voice!

I peeked out from around the tassel. Sure enough, my mom had just arrived on the scene, followed by Lark with—get this—her lap harp strapped across her back. Wow, this had suddenly turned into one of those bizarro scenes from a weird reality cable TV show.

I could see the commercial for it now: *Stayed tuned for this week's episode, as our miniboy on a tassel reunites with his strange but lovable family.*

"Dude, you've got to get out there," Pablo said. "Look at me."

When I turned to look at him, my nose bumped right into the tassel he was holding. He's a tricky little guy.

"Ticklish?" he said, swishing its floppy ends across my nose.

It did make my nose itch. I reached up to rub it, but he wouldn't let me.

"No rubbing," he said. "Only sneezing."

My nose started to twitch really bad.

"Ah . . . ah . . . ah . . ."

Even in my presneeze state, I could see Vu walking up to the group. He was carrying our diorama and looking really nervous. When he asked if anyone had seen me, Pablo got really serious about tickling me with the tassel.

"Come on, bro. We need you big!"

"Ah . . . ah . . . chooooo!"

Luckily, when I sneezed, everyone was talking to Vu, so they didn't see me shooting up from the middle of Mr. Quirk's shoe. It was as if I had appeared from nowhere and I was standing there, standard sixth-grade size, stomping on Mr. Quirk's right brown loafer.

"Ow," he said, "you're stepping on my toe."

"Sorry," I answered, backing off of his shoe. "I have a little problem with personal space. Sometimes I cross the line."

"Where did you come from?" Robin asked.

"The cafeteria," I said, without batting an eye. "Taco day."

"You left my office for a taco, Daniel?" Mr. Quirk said. "I specifically asked you to wait until I returned."

Oops. Think fast, Dan.

"Uh . . . I had to come find Vu and tell him I wasn't going to be able to do the presentation with him."

"That was a very responsible thing to do, sweetie," my mom said. "You have to be considerate of your friends."

"Mrs. Funk, I called you because I had received a report that Daniel has been acting . . . well . . . odd," Mr. Quirk said.

"Like that's anything new," Robin chimed in.

"He was talking aloud to himself when no one was there," Mr. Quirk said quietly to my mom.

I glanced over at Granny, and she gave me the keep-your-mouth-shut-I'll-handle-this look.

"He was following my instructions," Granny said.

"To talk to himself?" my mom asked.

"No, to practice. I told him to talk like an Egyptian all day. You want to be an Egyptian, you have to walk the walk, talk the talk. An actor boyfriend of mine once told me that if you wanted to play a cowboy, you had to live on the prairie and eat rattlesnake."

I think she had them agreeing with her, up until the rattlesnake part. She definitely lost them there. I jumped in to help.

"I've been pretending to be King Tut," I said. "In my imagination, I see my subjects all around me."

"Oh, this is so wonderfully creative, isn't it, Dirk?" Lola said. "Daniel is channeling the ancient Egyptians. This is what education is all about. Walking a mile in another's shoes."

I'll be honest with you.

I had no idea what Lola was talking about, but Mr. Quirk was nodding and smiling at her, so it worked for me. Wait a minute. He was smiling a little too much at her.

Holy macaroni! My principal has a crush on my grandmother.

It just doesn't get any grosser than that.

"Do you feel okay, honey?" my mom asked me.

"I'm totally fine, Mom." At least I was, until I saw Eyebrows Dirk flirting with Lola.

"Frankly, he seems fine to me, too," my mom said to Mr. Quirk. "And I am a medical doctor." She just didn't mention the fact that her patients are cats and dogs and cussing parrots.

"Perhaps I was overreacting," Mr. Quirk said. "It's just that Vince Bruno seemed very concerned and upset about Daniel."

"Vince Bruno!" Robin said. "No wonder! He's the guy competing against Daniel. Don't you see? He was trying to keep him away from the assembly!"

"That is so mean," her friend Jenna said.

"His dad's the guy who took away our uniform money," Robin said.

"That is so mean," Jenna said.

Hello? Earth to Jenna's brain. Anyone home?

"Wasn't there like a bunch of gold in King Tut's tomb?" Hailey asked.

"Silver, too," Vu said. "And jewels."

Hailey took off the silver earrings she was wearing and handed them to Vu.

"Here," she said. "Put these in your diorama. They'll look awesome. And by the way, cute hair."

Vu looked really happy. All that gel had finally paid off.

"Here, take my earrings too," Kimberly said. "Go beat that jerk. We're all rooting for you to win, aren't we, Robin?"

"For sure," said Robin. "I always tell Daniel what a winner he is."

Really? I guess she says it when I'm not around.

While Mr. Quirk got the kids in their seats for the assembly, Vu and I draped the girls' earrings over King Tut's coffin. I tried to cover up the part where Pablo had been. I was hoping Vu wouldn't notice that he was gone.

"Where's the mini-mummy?" Vu asked. So much for that hope.

I looked down at Mr. Quirk's loafer to see if I could figure out a way to pick up Pablo without looking weird.

Pablo was gone!

"I think he escaped," I said.

Vu laughed. What he didn't know was that I was telling the absolute truth.

CHAPTER 17

The Funkster's Funky Fact #17: The Egyptians thought it was good luck to enter a house with the left foot first.

Mr. Quirk introduced the finalists, and we walked onto the stage and took a seat. Vu handed me our diorama and I held it in my lap. Vince Bruno put his down on the table between us because it was too hot for him to hold. He had nuked it in the cafeteria microwave at lunch so it would be, as he said, a truly multisensory experience. It you ask me, and I know you didn't, his multisensory experience was letting off a pretty garlicky odor.

"Your diorama smells," I said.

"Yeah, well, yours stinks," he answered. "In more ways than one."

I noticed that he had put a brown paper bag about the size of a lunch sack on the table next to his diorama. I tried to see what was inside it. A side of meatballs? Free passes for everyone to Pizza King? I wouldn't put a cheap trick like that beyond Vince. He's the kind of guy who thinks his parents' money could win him the competition.

"What's in the bag?" I asked him.

"That's for me to know and you to find out," he said.

The Pizza Prince may be rich, but he sure isn't much on the clever comebacks.

While we were waiting to begin, I looked around the room for Pablo. There was no way I was going to find him. I could see Granny pacing back and forth. I knew she was nervous about Pablo. There were at least two hundred ways he could get squished in there. I was hoping he had jumped off Mr. Quirk's shoe and was hiding someplace safe until the presentation was over. I would have felt much better if I had known where he was.

My mom, Lola, and Lark had taken seats in the front row. Mr. Quirk was introduced us, then went and sat down in the front row too. He took the seat right next to Lola, even though there were about ten other empty seats that gave him a better view. I don't want to gross you out, but that was even further proof that he had a crush on her.

You know what? Let's not go there. Not now, not ever.

It was decided that Vu and I would go first. The Prince of Pizza told Mr. Quirk that he wanted to go last because of the "saving the best for last" thing. Vu and I got ourselves set up in the center of the stage, wished each other good luck, and high-fived.

"Bring it on," I said to him.

"Rock the house," he said to me.

And we began.

I don't want you to be tense about this, because we were tense enough for all of us. So let me just tell you right now that it couldn't have gone any better. We remembered all our lines and even added a few new ones. Not one sand crab came out to bite anyone in the behind. The girls in the audience thought the earrings were awesome. And the best part came during the question-and-answer session, when Brandon Ross wanted the gross details on how they made mummies back in ancient Egypt.

"Mummies were how Egyptians prepared the dead to go into the afterlife," Vu said. "After a person died, they took out his internal organs and wrapped the body in linen to preserve the mummy."

"The first thing they always did was take out the dead guy's brain, which they removed through the nostrils," I added, just for spice.

I knew that Brandon Ross, being the gross guy that he is, would love that little fact. But a lot of the other kids got really interested too. I mean, that's the kind of thing they just don't teach you in school.

About halfway through our presentation, a surprising thing happened. I don't know if it was a highlight or a lowlight. Actually, I take that back, it was definitely a lowlight. My sister Lark suddenly felt inspired to stand up from the audience, strap on her trusty lap harp, and come up on stage.

Now I know you're probably saying to yourself, "No, she didn't. That would be too weird." But the thing you have to know about Lark is that she thinks she's really talented and was doing Vu and me a favor to add a musical interlude to our presentation. That's how dense she is about herself. She thinks her poetry is great. She thinks everyone wants to go to her blog and hang on every little thought that runs through her twisted brain. And, unbelievable as it seems, she thinks she plays a wicked lap harp. Sisters. Go figure them out.

Anyway, now that you're over the shock of her strutting up there and serenading the school, I can tell you that she played an original tune (and I use the term loosely, because it had *no* tune at all) called "Mummy Dearest." It was . . . well . . . let's just say . . . highly unusual. If you're dying to know what it sounded like, you can check it out on cover-your-ears dot-com, but I don't recommend that, unless you're wearing earplugs and you've tested them to make sure absolutely no sound comes through.

Lola led the applause, and since all her students really like her, they kind of joined in. There was a second when I thought Lark might fire up the lap harp and do another song, but fortunately Lola escorted her off the stage so that Vu and I could do our big finish. After we were done, everybody applauded a lot. I could tell this irritated Vince Bruno no end.

"Your turn," I said to him. "Think you can top that?"

"It wasn't even multisensory," he said, like anyone cared about the odor coming from his shoe box. "If you turkeys want to see how it's done, just watch the Prince of Pizza."

He adjusted his tie (oh yeah, did I mention he was wearing a tie with little pizzas all over it) and walked to center stage, taking his brown paper bag with him. When he got there, he unfolded the top and reached inside.

You're not going to believe what was in there.

CHAPTER 18

The Funkster's Funky Fact #18:
The basic cheese pizza was designed to represent the
colors of the Italian flag—tomatoes for red,
cheese for white, and basil for green.

Yup. It was Pablo.

He was hanging on to some kind of black electronic device that was poking out of the top of the paper bag. I couldn't exactly see what it was at first.

Vince pulled the device out, unfolded it, and slipped it on his head. Oh wow. It was a microphone, the kind rock singers use at concerts so they can sing and still have their hands free to play the guitar. The top went over his hair, or I should say, the red fuzz that made his entire head look like a tomato. A round Ping-Pong ball–sized mic swiveled in front, so he could pull it right up to his mouth.

Perched on top of that mic, sprawled out flat so you couldn't see him if you didn't know he was there, was my twin brother, Pablo Picasso Diego Funk.

"Testing . . . one, two, three . . . testing," Vince said, and then blew into the mic to make sure it was working. That breath nearly blew Pablo onto the floor, but he grabbed on tight and dug his feet into the little holes on the mic's surface, just like they were toeholds on my geode.

If you're thinking that Vince knew Pablo was on the mic, forget it. It's a known fact that people can't see things that are right under their noses. Try it. Go ahead. Knock yourself out. Look straight down your nose. What do you see under there? Nothing, right?

And that's exactly what Vince Bruno saw when he looked down at his mic. Nothing. This will be an important fact for you to know about thirty seconds from now.

"You don't need to use that thing," Vu whispered to Vince. "This isn't a rock concert."

"This isn't a thing," Vince said. "It happens to be the UX 18 professional 16-channel wireless headset microphone, with belt pack and an operating range of two hundred and fifty feet."

"Like we care," I said.

"It cost two hundred and sixty-nine dollars," Vince said.

"Still no interest," I said. "Zero. Zip."

"My dad went out and bought it for me at lunch."

I have to confess I got a little twinge at that. Not that I wanted to have a dad with a lot of money. I just wanted to have a dad.

Vince blew into the mic one more time, cleared his throat, and began.

"My diorama is a multisensory experience that shows the invention of the world's greatest food, pizza. Oh, did I mention that my family owns Pizza King, which is how we get all of the money to buy really cool stuff like this microphone?"

A couple of kids groaned.

As Vince began his speech, Pablo climbed up to the top of the microphone, scaling it like he was rock climbing. When he got to the top, he was so close to Vince's mouth, it looked like he was going to crawl inside.

Pablo turned and flashed me the thumbs-up signal, but I still wasn't sure what he was up to.

"Pizza is one of our most popular dishes," Vince droned on. "It was invented in the Italian city of—"

"—*Stinky Bottom!*" a voice said. That was Pablo, talking into the microphone!

Everybody cracked up. Vince looked confused and completely shook up.

"I didn't say Stinky Bottom," he said. "I meant to say Naples. Pizza was invented in Naples."

What a brilliant plan. Pablo was going to plant words in the microphone that made Vince seem like the jerk he was. Vince would never know where they were coming from. Oh, this was genius. I could hardly wait to see what was coming next.

"The word pizza," Vince went on, straightening his tie, "comes from an old Italian word meaning—"

"—*to pass gas,*" Pablo said into the mic.

The kids howled. I howled. Vu howled. Even Mr. Quirk had to stifle a smile.

"I didn't say that!" Vince said.

"Then who did?" Alan Baker called out.

Mr. Tomato Head really looked like a tomato now. His face was as red as his hair. He tapped on the mic with his finger, just narrowly missing Pablo.

"Testing . . . one, two, three . . . testing."

Pablo was quiet, giving Vince the idea that whatever had gone wrong with the mic was fixed. Vince tried to continue.

"The first pizzas," he said, "consisted of flat bread covered with tomatoes, cheese, and—"

"—*boogers.*"

"Who said that?" Vince asked, whirling around to give me a dirty look.

"Not me," I said.

"Yeah well, I'm watching you, Funk."

He delivered his next line with one eye on the audience and one eye on me.

"The classic pizza is called Pizza Margherita. It was created by Raffaele Esposito for King Umberto and his lovely bride, whose name was Queen—"

"—*smelly armpits.*"

I couldn't help myself. I totally cracked up. This was too funny. Even Lark was laughing, and that's something that happens maybe once a year.

"It's him then, isn't it?" Vince said, pointing to Vu. "Shut up, man. I'm watching you."

I swear, you have never seen a face as red as Vince Bruno's had turned. I didn't feel sorry for him, though. Remember, this guy tripped me to destroy my diorama. That is not okay.

"Signor Esposito's pizzeria still exists today in Naples," he said, "and it's called—"

"—*The Barf Café and Puke Parlor.*"

The whole audience laughed like hyenas. I don't know if they thought Vu and I were saying those things, or if they thought Vince was doing it to be funny. But I can tell you this: Old Vince was not amused.

"That's it!" he said, pulling off his UX 18 professional 16-channel wireless headset microphone with belt pack. "I'm out of here. You guys can have your stupid diorama contest. It's lame anyway."

He stomped off the stage, down the stairs, and out of the auditorium.

"It appears that Mr. Bruno has experienced some technical difficulties," Mr. Stout said, coming up to the stage. "However, I think we should vote for the winner anyway."

He asked all the kids to applaud for the best diorama.

We won.

CHAPTER 19

The Funkster's Funky Fact #19: The average height of an NBA basketball player is six feet seven inches.

Vu's parents kept their word.

Two nights later, he and I were sitting in the Staples Center in downtown Los Angeles, which is about fifteen miles from the beach where we live. In case you don't know, it's the home of the Los Angeles Lakers basketball team.

Our seats were pretty high up, in the next-to-last row way at the top. But I didn't care. It was just so cool to be at my first-ever professional basketball game. Besides, I had brought my mom's bird-watching binoculars, and when I used them, I could see pretty well.

Not long after tip-off, there was an announcement over the loudspeaker.

"Attention, all Lakers fans."

Wait! I knew that voice.

"The Lakers organization is proud to announce that we have in the house tonight the winners of the Ocean Avenue Middle School Diorama Competition."

Pablo! How did he get here? Granny told him he couldn't go to the game.

I looked in my shirt pocket. Yup, there was a half-eaten root beer jelly bean, a sure sign that The Pablo had been there.

"Will Daniel Funk and Vu Tran please stand up and take a bow," the loudspeaker said. "The Lakers salute you! You are the real champions of the night!"

"This is unbelievable, man," Vu said. "How did they know?"

"Good question," I said.

As I took my bow and the crowd cheered, there were a million other questions racing through my mind. How did Pablo sneak out of the house? How did he get from my pocket to the announcer's booth? How did he take over the microphone?

Well, actually, I knew the answer to that one. I had seen him in action on a microphone, and he knew his way around one pretty well.

You're not going to believe what happened a few minutes later.

A man with a badge and an official Lakers shirt came over to us and said, "Come with me, boys."

I thought for sure Pablo had been caught, and this guy was taking us to jail or wherever they take one-inch-high kids who hijack announcers' microphones. But that's not where he took us.

Are you ready for this?

He took us courtside, to the first row of seats. Friends, I'm talking right behind the players' bench.

"Have a seat," the official dude said. "Enjoy the game."

"You mean we can actually sit here?" I asked.

"The owners want to congratulate you on your win," he said. "Just our team's way of saying 'good work.'"

A few minutes later, a purple and gold cardboard box arrived with all sorts of Lakers souvenirs. It had a pennant for each of us, and an autographed Lakers hat.

I couldn't believe this. It was the best night of my life. I picked up the hat to put it on, and what do you think I found underneath?

I'll give you three hints.

Number One: It's the size of the fourth toe on my left foot.

Number Two: It's not an *it*, it's a *he*.

And Number Three: He's the best little brother in the whole wide world.

CHAPTER 20

The Funkster's Funky Fact #20: Identical twins have almost identical brain-wave patterns.

Hey, it's The Pablo here.

Little brother, he says? Okay, maybe I'm small. But I'm older

than he is by thirty seconds. So I deserve the last word.

I bet you're wondering how I got to the announcer's booth.

And how I got into the Pizza Prince's

microphone bag.

Dudes, listen up: I can't tell you all my secrets.

But I'll tell you this: You can ride very far on a GUP's shoe.

Like The Pablo always says, why walk when you can ride?

I'll be back, Jack.

Until then, do your thing, chicken wing.

Love,

The Pablo

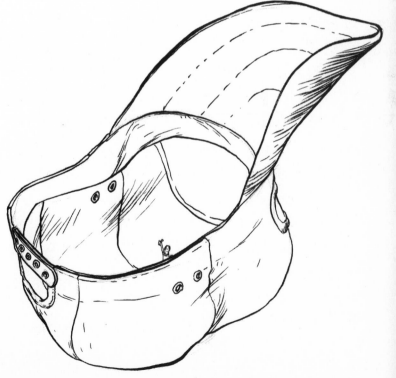

Lin Oliver is the coauthor, with Henry Winkler, of the *New York Times* bestselling Hank Zipzer series. She is the executive producer of the Nickelodeon series *Wayside* as well as the writer and producer of other movies, books, and television series for children and families. She cofounded the Society of Children's Book Writers and Illustrators, of which she is executive director. Lin lives in Los Angeles with her husband, three sons, and one overly frisky dog. Visit her on the Web at www.linoliver.com.

Stephen Gilpin is the illustrator of many books, including the Extraordinary Adventures of Ordinary Boy series written by William Boniface. He graduated from the School of Visual Arts in New York City, where he studied painting and cartooning. He lives in Tulsa, Oklahoma. Visit him on the Web at www.sgilpin.com.